SADISTIC SHERLOCK

JOCELYNN DRAKE
RINDA ELLIOTT

Jocelynn: To Dad, Thanks for starting a life-long love affair for Holmes and Watson.

Rinda: To Robert, for the constant support and belief in what I do. To Rachel, for listening when the self-doubt monster attacks and for being willing to plot at the drop of a hat. To Jocelynn, because I love working with you and the friendship we've formed is priceless!

THE WARD SECURITY SERIES

Psycho Romeo
Dantès Unglued
Deadly Dorian
Jackson (a novella)
Sadistic Sherlock

ALSO BY JOCELYNN DRAKE AND RINDA ELLIOTT

The Unbreakable Bonds Series

Shiver

Shatter

Torch

Devour

Blaze

Unbreakable Bonds Short Story Collection

Unbreakable Stories: Lucas

Unbreakable Stories: Snow

Unbreakable Stories: Rowe

Unbreakable Stories: Ian

ALSO BY JOCELYNN DRAKE

The Dark Days Series

Bound to Me

The Dead, the Damned and the Forgotten

Nightwalker

Dayhunter

Dawnbreaker

Pray for Dawn

Wait for Dusk

Burn the Night

The Lost Night

Stefan

The Asylum Tales

The Asylum Interviews: Bronx

The Asylum Interviews: Trixie

Angel's Ink

Dead Man's Deal

Demon's Vengeance

Ice & Snow Christmas Series

Walking on Thin Ice

Ice, Snow, & Mistletoe

ALSO BY RINDA ELLIOTT

Beri O'Dell Series

Dweller on the Threshold

Blood of an Ancient

The Brothers Bernaux

Raisonne Curse

Sisters of Fate

Foretold

Forecast

Foresworn

The Kithran Regenesis Series

Kithra

Replicant

Catalyst

Origin

Crux Survivors Series

After the Crux

Sole Survivors

This book is a work of fiction. Names, characters, places, and incidents are products of the authors' imaginations or are used factiously and are not to be construed as real. Any resemblance to actual events, locales, or organizations, or persons, living or dead, is entirely coincidental.

SADISTIC SHERLOCK. Copyright ©2018 Jocelynn Drake and Rinda Elliott. All rights reserved under International and Pan-American Copyright Conventions. By payment of the required fees, you have been granted the nonexclusive, nontransferable right to access and read the text of this e-book on-screen. No part of this text may be reproduced, transmitted, introduced into any information storage and retrieval system, in any form or by any means, whether electronic or mechanical, now known or hereinafter invented, without the express written permission of Jocelynn Drake and Rinda Elliott.

Cover art by Stephen Drake of Design by Drake.

Copyedited and proofed by Flat Earth Editing.

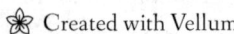 Created with Vellum

CHAPTER ONE

Dominic Walsh had always dreamed of being on a movie set. Growing up, he'd loved action movies with lots of explosions, car chases, and brutal fistfights. He'd sneaked into tons of theaters, the darkness swallowing him up while a bigger, more exciting world flickered on the screen in front of him. It all seemed so much more glamorous and thrilling than anything he would be doing with his life.

The reality, he discovered, was a massive disappointment. This... was boring as fuck.

A major film production company had swept into Cincinnati to film some scenes for a new movie, and Ward Security had been hired to add an extra layer of protection for some of the actors. The local police and a second security company kept the fans and lookie-loos at bay. The situation became particularly dire when the lead actor started receiving death threats from a persistent stalker.

Dom was spending most of his time acting as Trent Elrige's dark shadow. The guy was putting up an impressive front that he wasn't scared shitless about the stalker. He had that perfect George Clooney smile, the dreamy Brad Pitt eyes, and the "I'm just a normal kind of guy" personality of Chris Pratt. But there had been a few moments when he'd forgotten that Dom was following him. He'd let his guard down and stared off into space, his hand shaking slightly at his side as if the world were crashing down on him.

Poor fucker.

Did he even know what normal was anymore? He left his trailer to hit the set, and fans would scream his name. He'd travel from the set to his hotel and people would scream, demanding an autograph or a selfie. Ward Security put a hard stop to all selfies until the stalker was caught. They were too dangerous.

So far, Trent was following all their rules, and it was a relief that he was at least taking the threat seriously. Of course, the intense schedule the guy was keeping with the shooting, interviews, and trying to make time for his fans while in addition having some private time, meant that Rowe was keeping them on a strict rotation. No bodyguard was allowed to put in more than eight hours shifts. He wanted his people to stay sharp.

Right now, Dom was on rotation with Sven and Garrett—two of his coworkers at Ward Security—which made him laugh. Somehow Sven had drawn the short stick and was on the third shift. He could imagine Sven's boyfriend Geoffrey throwing a massive fit. He didn't have his giant Viking to snuggle with at night, and Sven wasn't allowed to get any pictures, autographs, or sneak Geoffrey in to meet Trent.

Of course, Sven likely found ways to distract Geoffrey from his poor mood. The sexy elfin blond might not be happy about this job, but his love for Sven would never waver. The two men were made for each other, and Dom couldn't help but feel a little envious.

He'd done the partying and sleeping around thing for a while. He'd had his fun. Hell, he'd thought he'd be having that kind of fun for a few more years, but then Abe Stephens stepped into his life, and well...plans were meant to be changed.

Maybe.

Abe wasn't giving him a whole hell of a lot to work with. They'd been texting for months. Met up for dinner a few times. Dom had been careful to keep it all casual and fun. But every time he mentioned maybe something more, Abe would shy away. He gave every sign that he was interested, but something was holding him back. Was it the age thing? Or that he was a guy?

Dom ran a hand over this face. He needed to focus on the job. Every time his mind drifted to something else, it was Abe who was dancing through his brain. If he fucked up this job, Rowe was going to skin him alive. *Screw Rowe, he'd never forgive himself.* He was good at protection. He just needed to focus.

"Girl trouble?" Trent's deep voice broke into his thoughts.

Dom looked up at Trent who was standing next to the mini bar, grabbing two bottles of water from the tiny fridge. They were in a conference room on the second floor of a hotel downtown. Trent had been needed for filming for only a few hours in the morning. After a massage and lunch that consisted of a ridiculous amount of protein, they'd retired to the conference room for a series of interviews before Trent had to be back on the set that night.

"More like guy trouble," Dom corrected him.

Trent stared at him, confused for a second, before understanding hit him like a bolt of lightning. His mouth bobbed once before he finally said, "I couldn't tell. I mean—oh! No, I mean, that's cool."

Dom laughed loudly, rocking back on his heels. The poor guy's face was so damn red with embarrassment. He'd never seen Trent Elrige fluster. The actor was smooth as silk with everyone he talked to; he made it seem like everything he did was intentional. Dom had just caught him so off guard that he couldn't cover it.

"Dude, it's fine," Dom said when he finally stopped laughing. "Yeah, I'm gay. And dating is that same kind of minefield shitstorm for us too."

Trent snorted. "Tell me about it."

Dom watched as a look of longing crossed over Trent's face for a moment, the water forgotten in his hands. But then he shook his head and smiled crookedly at Dom. Yeah, there was definitely a story there. Was Trent in the closet? Or was it that he cared for someone he was having trouble snagging because of his complicated life? Ooooooh, Dom was dying to ask him. Digging around in Trent's life would be such a great distraction from his own worries about Abe. But he kept his mouth shut. From what he could see, Trent's privacy was pretty much nonexistent. If he managed to keep a secret or two to himself, then Dom was happy to let him have them.

"I've always kind of wondered," Trent started again. "Is dating hard when you're working security? I've got some friends who have personal security on their payroll. They travel with them and spend a lot of time together. Not much time for dating."

Dom shrugged, accepting the bottle of water from Trent when he held one out toward him. "I haven't done much long-term dating while working security. More of the short-term, 'gone by morning' kind of thing." Trent chuckled and flopped down in one of the cushioned chairs around the small coffee table. "But this guy...he's different. We've been friends for a bit, and he's got a good understanding of the crazy schedule I have. We text and sometimes grab a bite to eat. Nothing big."

"But you would like something a little bigger? Maybe breakfast?"

Dom huffed a laugh. Breakfast the next morning with Abe after a night of great sex? Yeah, that sounded like a big slice of heaven. He couldn't imagine where things would lead with Abe, but he'd like to at least have the chance to try.

"Breakfast sounds pretty good to me," Dom agreed.

Trent sat up in his chair and placed his unopened bottle of water on the table in front of him. "I know you don't know me. I'm just some lucky schmuck who occasionally pretends to be a cop or a CEO or a super spy, but in those rare moments when I get to be a real human being, I regret all those times I didn't at least push for a little something more. Even if it all blew up in my face, at least I would have known."

"I should ask for breakfast?" Dom asked with a wide grin.

Trent snorted. "You might consider asking for dinner and a movie first, then see where it goes."

"I'll give that a try. But first, you've got an interview starting soon with some reporter from *Vogue*. Or was it *Cosmo*? You gonna provide your top ten list of sexual positions?"

Trent winked at him and gave his patented movie-star smile that he whipped out when the fans were about. Dom noticed that he'd tried the smile on him only one time when they first met and then promptly stopped when Dom had established that he was the law. "You need some new techniques to add to your repertoire?"

"Oh, no. I'm good. Real good," Dom teased, drawing out the last two words.

Trent laughed, and Dom shook his head. At least the guy had some time to relax before yet another interview. A knock at the door cut off Trent's laugh, and Dom went to answer it. Their fun was over for now.

Opening the door only part of the way, Dom gave his best glare down at the young woman in the business suit with a large bag over her shoulder. She held out a badge that contained her press credentials. It all matched the information Trent's assistant had forwarded over to Ward Security that morning.

With a grunt, he handed back the badge and moved out of the doorway so she could enter. "I need to check your bag," he said, keeping his body between her and the path to Trent.

Her face twisted in a look of shock and anger. "They checked my bag in the lobby."

"*They* checked it. Not me." He waved his fingers at her. "Hand it over or no interview."

She huffed and pouted but still handed over the bag while muttering under her breath. He ignored her shitty attitude, quickly searching through a bag that contained her wallet, lipstick, four pens, an iPad, a condom, and a tampon. At least she was prepared for just about anything. Without comment, he handed the bag back and ushered her around the corner, past the medium-sized conference room table to the two padded chairs and coffee table.

Trent stood and warmly greeted her, apologizing for the added security precautions, which she smoothly brushed aside. For him, she was understanding and compassionate. Dom was just the help. Catching Trent's gaze just past the reporter's shoulder, Dom rolled his eyes and made a strangling motion. Trent smirked at him before directing the reporter to sit down so they could start the interview.

Another knock at the door had him frowning at Trent.

"That should be the refreshments I ordered for the interview," the actor said, wincing a little when he realized that he'd forgotten to tell Dom. "I called down to the front desk this morning and set it up."

Dom's heart slowed down again, and he turned toward the door. Peeking out, there was a man in the hotel livery with a cart covered in a white tablecloth. There were several dishes under silver covers and a bouquet of red roses.

"What's on the cart?" he demanded.

"Um…j-just some fruits and a cheese and cracker tray," the guy stammered. "Somebody placed the order this morning for it to be delivered at this time."

Dom stepped out of the way and motioned for the man to enter the room with the cart. "Set it up over there at the end of the conference table."

The guy paused and stared at Trent for a moment, who was busy answering a question the reporter had just asked about his current project. "I think it would be better over there."

"No." Dom started to approach the hotel staff member, aiming to put his body firmly between Trent and this idiot when he saw him wrap his fingers around a knife far larger than what was needed to slice cheese or fruit. *Goddammit!* This was the stalker.

The man screamed and charged Trent, but Dom grabbed one arm, swinging him away from the actor. The woman's panicked screech filled the room, but Dom didn't look from the man who crashed into the cart, knocking it over. He immediately rolled back to his feet and dropped into a fighter's stance, the knife still firmly clutched in his right hand.

"Get out of the way, Strawberry Shortcake!" the attacker snarled.

"Are you shitting me with this?" He'd heard the nickname more than enough growing up. He thought reaching over six feet tall and two hundred pounds of pure muscle would fix things so no one dared to utter it again. But this asshat was obviously out of his mind.

The attacker took a swipe at Dom, the sharp edge slicing dangerously through the air. Dom dodged the blade and countered by smashing his fist into the guy's jaw. On a second swipe, Dom managed to hit a pressure point in his wrist. The knife clattered uselessly to the ground and the man stepped back, undeterred.

"Call security!" Dom shouted. He had this guy handled, but they'd need the police in there to take the asshole away as well as to question the hell out of the hotel to figure out how he got in.

"Do you want me—" Trent started to offer, but Dom cut him off.

"Just call for backup and stay away from this douchecanoe!"

"I'm going to fucking kill you, Trent Elrige! You ruined my marriage!" the attacker screamed. He tried to charge around Dom to get at Trent again, but Dom remained firmly in his path. They traded blows, the man again surprising Dom with his fight training. The guy knew his shit, but Dom was better. The bastard stumbled back, wiping some blood off his mouth. There was an ugly look to his eyes, as if he was only too happy to kill Dom if it meant getting his hands on Trent. He took one step and Dom kicked him square in the chest, sending him reeling backward.

The man's large frame crashed through the plate glass window. Dom ran to the opening to see he'd hit the roof of a parked taxi cab one floor below. People outside the hotel screamed and panicked. Cops nearby rushed to the man, who groaned but didn't try to get up.

"Holy shit!" Trent said, standing next to him.

Dom grabbed his arm and quickly ushered him deep into the room where the windows were darkened, and people couldn't see him any longer.

The door to the room slammed open. Garrett and three cops ran inside. Dom kept his body positioned in front of Trent while pushing him back against the wall. There was too much chaos, and the room was no longer secure.

Trent placed a gentle hand on Dom's shoulder and squeezed. "I'm good. We're all good. You saved my life."

"Garrett! Secure the room!" Dom shouted. He was relieved to hear that Trent was okay, but he wasn't ready to stand down. Not until the cops had the attacker in custody and the room was locked down.

In a matter of seconds, the reporter was ushered out. Cops stood in front of the window and the door. A couple of detectives took their statements about the events before leaving to descend on the hotel's management. A flurry of activity that kept Dom's adrenaline pumping hard through his body.

It was only when he and Garrett were up in Trent's luxurious suite that he felt himself starting to crash. The incident had gotten Trent excused from filming that night and the rest of his interviews rescheduled for another day. The movie star was stretched out in a pair of lounge pants and a T-shirt, a beer clutched tightly in one hand.

Dom looked up when Garrett walked back in from the balcony, sliding his cell phone into his pocket. The handsome bodyguard grinned at him. "The boss says you did a good job."

"A good job?" Trent scoffed, popping his head up. "The guy's a freaking hero. *He kicked a man out a window!*"

"Yeah, they're already talking about that back at the office."

"I can't even do that without breakaway glass," Trent muttered, seeming a little disappointed in his skills, now that he'd seen the real thing in person.

Dom grinned at Trent. The guy was really starting to grow on him. "I've seen your movies. You've done plenty of really cool things."

"Don't patronize me, Strawberry Shortcake," Trent said, pointing his beer bottle at Dom. "You're a goddamn hero."

"Just doing my job. The boss said to protect you at any cost. That includes defenestration."

"Defene-what?" Garrett said.

"Defenestration. It means to throw out a window."

Trent chuckled. "You're weird."

"You're also off the clock," Garrett added. "I've got things covered until Sven comes on shift at midnight. Though I imagine you've done all the hard work, and things are going to be pretty quiet."

Trent lurched into an upright position, nearly spilling his beer down the front of his T-shirt, and grinned at Dom. "Stay. We'll drink and order up some of the biggest steaks we can get our hands on in this city. No more fans or reporters. We'll just bullshit and drink."

For a heartbeat, Dom actually considered it. Trent Elrige was, deep down, a nice guy who could probably use a friend he could trust. And Dom was seriously flattered that he would consider him for the position. But Trent's advice was still ringing in his head.

"I'd like to, but you gave me some advice earlier, and I'd really like to see if I can get that breakfast. Raincheck?"

Trent's smile turned a little bittersweet, but he nodded. "Absolutely."

Garrett was giving Dom a look like he'd lost his fucking mind, but he just winked at his friend, knowing he'd have to explain later.

He pushed to his feet and Trent suddenly slammed his beer on the table and hurried over to the desk. He scribbled something down on a piece of paper and tore it off. When he handed it over, Dom was shocked to find that it was a phone number. It was very likely Trent's personal cell phone number. He was holding the personal cell number for an A-list celebrity. *Holy. Fucking. Shit.*

"Before I forget. I'm only in town for a few more days, and I want to hear about your breakfast." Trent paused and gave a self-deprecating little roll of his eyes. "You know, so I can live vicariously through you."

"You'll get there."

Trent smiled. "Thanks again, Strawberry Shortcake."

"Fucking hack," Dom muttered and then threw Trent one last grin before leaving with the number in his pocket.

By the time he reached the elevator, Dom had pulled up Abe's contact information on his cell phone.

D: I just turned down Trent Elrige for a date. Poor guy. He was crushed.

He quickly checked through a couple of other messages from his coworkers and cleaned out some spam email that had arrived during the day. He was just about to put his phone into his pocket again when a message from Abe pinged through.

A: Why would you do such a damn fool thing?

D: No more hit movies, no more sweaty tattoos on the big screen. He's retiring to lick his wounds. I've deprived the world of an international treasure.

A: I bow down to your powers of heartbreak.

Dom paused and licked his lips. Nothing ventured, nothing gained.

D: Instead, how about you come over to my place for celebratory tacos and I tell you how I pretended to be a superhero today?

He waited. His damn heart was pounding harder than when he'd fought Trent's would-be killer. What if Abe said no? It wouldn't be the first time, but Dom felt like he was getting down to the last of his chances with Abe. He didn't want to push the guy, but he also didn't want to be strung along with no hope.

The elevator chimed as it reached the lobby. Dom started to put his phone away when a message popped up.

A: What should I bring?

CHAPTER TWO

Abe Stephens set down his phone and pressed his forehead against the wall. He groaned long and loud. Flirting with danger seemed to be his M.O. more and more these days. It was getting too damn hard to resist Dominic Walsh. He was hands down one of the sexiest men he'd ever met. One chime from his phone and he was hurriedly pulling up the app, hoping it was Dom with his funny texts. Some of which left him feeling faintly sweaty and tempted to go back on his vow to start looking for someone who'd be interested in a more permanent arrangement rather than the wild, string-free fling he was sure Dom was looking for.

It was worse when they actually spoke.

Fuck, he loved Dom's voice. Warm, scratchy, and always tinged with humor. The kind of voice that made him think of sweat-pants Sundays, curled up on the couch in front of an action movie. Or low, gritty murmurs and moans of pleasure in a dark room.

As usual, whenever he let his mind go there, he lost track of anything else he was doing. He had a feeling that voice would sound so good in the dark, it would make him lose his mind. He blinked at the wall, desperate to swing his imagination away from that.

Why the hell had he agreed to go to Dom's house? His *home*!

Abe snatched the towel off his shoulder and wiped at the sweat over his brow. The late-June heat was making the humid air thick. He began unplugging tools in his garage. If he was going to continue to work here, he should probably think about putting in air conditioning. He'd taken up creating hand-carved chairs as a hobby, then moved into whimsical window frames after a neighbor had commissioned one for his daughter's eighth birthday. Nearly every parent who'd attended the little girl's party had called to order more, and several had gone on to order chairs as well. Word had spread.

At this rate, he could quit the accounting he did part-time altogether.

Though that was his profession, he hadn't truly enjoyed it since the financial world had gone to shit in 2008.

With his workshop put to rights, he walked through his house for a shower, telling himself with every step that he was just getting clean to be polite after sweating his ass off in his garage most of the day. He wasn't hoping that Dom would put his hands on his clean skin. Or press his face into his clean neck. Or nibble his way along his jaw to his lips while sliding his hands down his chest to his...fuck, he was going to need to take care of something else while he was in the shower.

Still calling himself a liar forty minutes later, his headlights lit up the cute white brick house he'd been to only once before. The place had surprised him. He'd expected to find Dom in an apartment or an in-town rental. Instead, Dom had invested in an older fixer-upper with lots of personality. Just like the man himself.

Set back in the trees, the house offered privacy on the quaint, heavily wooded street in Mount Airy, not far from the Mount Airy Forest. Dom had told him he bought the place for the old brick-arched doorway leading to the deck and for the backyard full of trees.

Dom surprised him every time he saw him. He came off as a jokester, but there were layers to the man Abe ached to explore.

He parked in the driveway and sat for another moment to

mentally put up thick walls around his heart. Tonight, it would be more difficult than usual because Abe had a big birthday coming up. The dreaded five-oh. He'd been dealing with a lot of deep thoughts about his life and where it was going. With his son happily settled down, he felt like he was drifting, and he wasn't sure why. He had everything he could possibly want. Happy son. A home. A fulfilling hobby. Steady income. What more could he possibly need?

His restlessness was at an all-time high, and Dom's determination to move beyond friendship was starting to wear him down. Not that he was *that* resistant—he wasn't—it was just…he couldn't get why someone as insanely hot as Dominic Walsh wanted him so badly.

A lot of those deep thoughts lately had been the "What would naked with Dom be like?" kind….

Fuck, he didn't know what to do about Dom. His own flip-flopping thoughts were driving him nuts. Dom was a player. No doubt about it. Abe had enjoyed a few one-night stands following his divorce from his wife years ago, but he wasn't interested in hooking up these days. He'd never really enjoyed casual sex. He liked having an emotional attachment to the person. To wake up the next morning and smile to see them lying on the other pillow, just waiting to make plans to see each other again.

But being in a near-constant state of arousal around Dom was driving him insane. Of course, this state wasn't new—not since Dom had spent a few days guarding him last year. Dom didn't seem to feel shirts were always necessary, and his years of training and martial arts had honed his body into a ripped fighting machine.

Attraction to men wasn't a new experience for Abe either. His first boner had arrived in the boys' gym locker room, his second while watching cheerleaders practicing the very next day. He'd known he was bisexual before a lot of people believed it was a real sexuality.

But then he'd met Patricia and fallen so hard that he hadn't looked anywhere else for a long, long time. After she stomped all over his heart, he just hadn't been able to dredge up much interest in sex outside of a hookup here and there.

And he'd yet to know what one of those was like with a man.

But he wanted to.

Badly.

The problem was...he was too nervous to try. He was too damn old to be fumbling around during sex. He knew what he liked when it came to his own body, but he had no clue what to do with another man. All he knew was what he craved...what he liked to watch when it came to porn.

And since Dom had been laying the charm on so thick, there had been so. Much. Porn. It was almost like he was seventeen again.

Almost.

"Abe?"

He raised his gaze to find those green eyes narrowed above a sexy-as-fuck grin in his open truck window.

"We having a truck picnic or did you want to come inside?" His smile faded as he stepped back and opened the door. "Just tacos and a movie. Promise."

Feeling like a fool, Abe got out and stood staring down at Dom, who looked just as edible in casual jeans and a ratty Nine Inch Nails tee as he did in the tight nightclub clothes Abe had seen him in last. While he wasn't bulky, his martial arts training and workouts had made his body into a tight thing of beauty with arms that rippled with muscle. *Those damn arms.* Abe's mouth watered, and his dick began to fill.

Dammit.

He cleared his throat, mumbled something about being hungry, and strode up the few steps to Dom's deck and front door—the whole time trying, without success, to talk his hard-on down.

Seemed his dick didn't have the same issues with self-confidence.

∽

Dom noticed the boner right away. The boner and the way Abe's gaze had been glued to his arms. He'd forgotten about the man's fascination with them. When he'd briefly taken Abe on as a client to protect him the year before, Abe hadn't hidden the direction of his gaze well. Dom had been one hundred percent open to hooking up with the hottest damn silver fox he'd ever seen in his life. Tall and broad-chested, Abe held this sort of solid carriage and big-guy sex appeal Dom hadn't even known he liked before.

But Abe wasn't biting.

And nothing he did seemed to work. He'd never had to try so hard to get laid.

It was humbling. His ego had definitely taken a beating. He'd been a little shameless at first, doing everything but parading around naked in front of the man. But their age difference really seemed to matter to Abe, so he'd backed down and tried to settle for friendship. Too bad the chemistry and his own running mouth made him forget sometimes.

But he'd never push where he wasn't wanted.

Problem was...he could tell he was. This wasn't the first boner he'd spotted on the guy. That was what made it so frustrating.

One of Dom's closest friends was dating Abe's son, Shane. When Dom had been called in when Shane got into some nasty shit, he'd been expecting to see someone more like his own father. Or how his father had looked before Dom had cut his family from his life. But Abe had been a teen dad, and now he was the epitome of sexy with his salt-and-pepper curly hair and close beard. Dom had lost sleep thinking about those big hands and the smile that somehow made him look both shy and forceful at the same time.

Like he wanted to pin Dom down and do all kinds of raunchy things to his body and he didn't know how to feel about that.

Dom had never wanted something so badly in his life. He wanted to experience every dirty and not-so-dirty thing that crossed Abe's mind.

That was what had him so mixed up. Dom was comfortable with Abe, but the man also made him feel young and awkward. *He was thirty-two fucking years old!* He wanted to wake up to coffee and donuts with him, but he also wanted to tug him into the shower and explore every inch of his masculine body with soapy hands.

"Go on in," he told Abe, who had stopped politely at the door.

Abe opened the door and held it open for Dom. "So, why aren't you out with Trent Elrige?"

Dom shrugged. "Because I wanted tacos. Got them from Cubitt's on the way home, so they're hot and fresh."

The low laugh that followed his words made him smile. So did the scent of freshly showered man and cologne as Dom passed through the doorway, his body brushing against Abe's. Dom's heart picked up beats. The man had put on *cologne*. That meant something. Subtle and musky...and holy shit, he smelled so good, Dom pulled the scent deep into his lungs. It was there—the desire.

Be patient. Be patient. Be patient.

The chant went through his head as they grabbed the food and some beers, then settled onto the couch in the living room. He clicked on the television. One of the Marvel movies blasted across the big screen, and Dom settled in, determined to enjoy a couple of hours of laughter and excitement because they both loved the franchise.

"This one has to be your favorite because of the helicopter and the arms, right?" he asked as he unwrapped the first fragrant taco. Cumin, thyme, chili powder, peppers, and lime. He took a deep breath and a big bite. He had this particular truck on an actual app on his phone, so he knew where it would be parked anytime he craved the spicy, shredded pork and fresh veggies. Juice dripped down his chin.

Abe laughed, handed him a napkin, and dug into the bag of food. "So, you were guarding Trent Elrige? What's he like?"

Dom shrugged. "Normal guy outside of being too good-looking to be real. We had an eventful night."

"How's that?"

"His stalker showed, but the situation was defused."

"Why do I get the feeling you're downplaying what happened?" Abe took a bite of his taco and groaned his pleasure.

Oh God, those kinds of noises would kill him. "I am a bit. I kicked the guy through a window. I'm sure Rowe will be happy to fight that bill with the hotel since they let the dumbass into the building." He spoke of his boss with fondness. There was no one who liked to argue as much as Rowe. He'd probably give Dom points for creativity.

"Dom?"

"Yeah?"

"You actually kicked a guy through a window?"

"I did. It was cool as shit."

Abe threw back his head, laughing once again. He did that a lot around Dom, and he found himself doing whatever he could to keep that sound coming. Abe had a deep, warm laugh that sent shivers through Dom.

"I wish I could have seen that." He turned back to the movie. "Oh, I love this part."

Dom settled in to watch, stealing glances at Abe throughout the movie. He realized he enjoyed this just as much as he would getting the man into his bed. There was an ease to them that was just as appealing as the heat.

At one point, Dom realized Abe was staring, and he shot him a wink. "So, Quinn was telling me that you're going on vacation with him and Shane next month. Brave man. Do you want to hear what I've walked in on at the office?"

"Fuck no," Abe growled with a shudder. "I'm happy for my son. Thrilled, really. But I'm not going with them. They only invited me because I was there for dinner when the topic came up. I plan to have a last-minute job."

Dom paused while twisting off the cap of his third beer. "Aw, they'd be good with the daddy there."

He rolled his eyes. "Don't you start with that daddy stuff again."

"But it's soooo hot," Dom drawled. He leaned closer. "Did you look at that porn link I sent?"

He expected red to creep into Abe's face, but instead he just lifted his eyebrow and gave Dom the naughtiest grin he'd ever seen on the man. "I watched the whole thing."

Dom waited. Partly out of curiosity and partly because he was slightly punch-drunk off that grin and the wicked promise in it. When Abe didn't say anything else, he groaned. "Come on, you can't leave it like that. Did you like it?"

"It was…interesting. Hot, yeah, but I don't think it's really my thing." He started to take a drink of his own beer and stopped. "But if it's yours, that's cool."

Rolling his eyes, he faced the movie again. He'd been sending different links to the man in the hopes of finding out just what did do it for him.

Again, he worried he was losing his touch when it came to seduction because, *damn*. Not that he'd resorted to sending porn links in the past.

"Those two are way too new to have 'the dad' tagging along," Abe continued, going back to the vacation topic. "Plus, it's a small cabin." He crossed one ankle over his knee, leaning back. "They could use the time away together. They both work long hours. There's no Wi-Fi there, so Quinn will basically have one thing to keep him from climbing the walls."

Dom winced at the thought of what his coworker and friend, Quinn, would be doing then with his boyfriend, Shane. Those two got pretty kinky, and he was only mostly guessing. *Mostly*. He'd caught Quinn being very toppy one night when they'd all gone out for drinks. Kid had surprised him. "Yeah, I can see why you wouldn't want to go." He took a swig of his beer. "Quinn said you desperately needed a vacation. Why's that?"

A funny expression crossed Abe's face, one Dom had trouble reading. Kind of like sheepish guilt and it had him intrigued instantly.

"What did you do?" he asked, his mind zinging in a dozen different directions. Abe was so straight-laced and pulled together that he was sure that man was hiding the wildest, dirtiest thoughts from the rest of the world. And he desperately wanted at that dirty side. He wanted it more than his next fucking orgasm.

Abe shrugged. "Nothing."

"Come on. It's gotta be something, or you wouldn't look like you just got caught in public with your pants down."

Abe glowered at him. "Have you ever noticed most of your conversations usually end up with some kind of nakedness?"

"I like naked." He waggled his brows. "I wish you'd let me show you a few things about how fun naked with a man can be."

As soon as the words left his lips, he knew he'd screwed up. Abe had never said being with a man would be a new thing for him, but Dom could tell. Well, he was guessing. But that very first night in his house, he'd caught the man surreptitiously eyeing him with actual blushes passing over his cheeks and neck, curiosity bright in his gaze. Outside of his killer body and that intriguing shy smile, those blushes made Dom a little crazy. He'd squirmed the whole night in Abe's spare bedroom.

He watched him now. Watched him shift on the cushions and look everywhere but at Dom. He stared at the beer in his hand, stomach twisting.

Dom sighed. "Hey, Abe. I'm sorry. If I promise to stop pushing, can we still be friends?"

That made the brown eyes lock back on him. "That's not in danger, Dominic. We'll be friends a long time. I...like you." He cleared his throat. "Quinn probably thinks I need a vacation because I've been talking about making some big changes in my life. I'm sure he thinks I'm in the midst of a midlife crisis."

"Are you?"

"I'm starting to wonder," Abe murmured as he looked away.

"What kinds of changes?"

"Not any I'm ready to talk about. I'm still mulling things over."

Abe shrugged and wiped the condensation off the side of his beer with a napkin before setting the bottle down on a coaster. Dom hadn't even realized he had coasters until Abe had pulled them out.

His heart gave a pang when he realized Abe really wasn't going to share his thoughts. He never did about anything important, and that more than anything let him know he had a long way to go—even when it came to their friendship.

But Abe was here and he was laughing and he'd put on *actual cologne*.

There was hope.

CHAPTER THREE

Dom was practically whistling to himself as he walked through the front doors of Ward Security the next morning.

"You're looking happier than usual," Karen commented as he entered the reception area. Her wide grin turned a little wicked. "I'm sure it has nothing to do with that sexy Trent Elrige singing your praises on the news last night."

Dom nearly stumbled a step at the mention of the movie star and asked who she was talking about. He recovered quickly, flashing the receptionist his patented easy grin. "Just another normal day for Ward Security."

Karen sighed dreamily. "Maybe. But he is so sexy. I mean, that smile and his hair." She sighed again. "You think he's looking for an older wife? Or even an older lover? I'd be happy to teach him a few things."

A choking noise jumped from his throat, and he was saved from having to say something by the ringing phone. He just waved as she answered and breathed a sigh of relief when he continued on to the main area. Trent might be a good-looking man, but he didn't hold a candle to Abe. Not that he was going to tell Karen that. Or anyone, for that matter. Nope, this was his secret as he struggled to find a way to convince the older man that he was worth a chance.

As he walked past the reception area, he was hit with a wall of chaotic sound. And it was like coming home. Seth and Sven were sparring, sending up loud smacks of skin hitting the vinyl foam mats. Garrett was over in another corner, chatting with Gidget, his arms flailing as he told her a story. Noah was hitting the heavy bag. He must have caught everyone before they left for jobs because so many of the security agents weren't usually here on weekdays.

"Hey!" Rowe's voice cut above the din, and everyone stopped. Dom looked up to find his boss leaning over the railing on the second floor, where most of the offices were located. "Has anybody heard from Andrei? My calls are going straight to voice mail."

"The ultrasound was today," Noah shouted back. He pushed some sweaty brown curls from his face and smiled up at his lover.

Dom stood at the foot of the stairs. Andrei Vallois was their COO, but he'd started out as a security agent like the rest of them. Just six months ago, he'd married billionaire Lucas Vallois. After a bit of searching, they'd located a surrogate and started to build their own family.

"I know that! The appointment was an hour ago."

Noah laughed. "Babe, it's too early to know the sex of the baby."

Rowe threw up his hands and stomped off, muttering something to himself before disappearing into his office.

Shaking his head, Dom climbed the stairs. As part of his usual routine, he paused in the second-floor kitchenette to make himself a cup of coffee with his favorite Mr. Rogers mug before wandering down to Rowe's office. He peeked in and found the man pacing behind his desk with his cell phone to his ear. He raised his hand to knock when Rowe swore and tossed his phone down on his desk.

"Hey, Dom," Rowe said, motioning for him to enter.

Rowan Ward was a strange man, but Dom respected the hell out of his boss. A former Army Ranger, Rowe had built the company up with a little help from his close friend Lucas, and it was now one of the premier security companies in the entire country. But it was more than Ward Security being on the cutting edge of surveillance and protection technology. Rowe had made the company into a close family. They were always there for each other, no matter what the cost or danger.

"You worried about the baby's health, Boss?" Dom asked, leaning his shoulder against the doorframe.

"Nah. That baby has got Andrei's genes. She's gonna be a fighter. I just want to hear if Lucas lost his shit when he saw his baby for the first time."

"She? You think it's a girl?"

Rowe clapped his hands together and rubbed them like he was cooking up some wicked plot. "Oh, yeah. Lucas and Andrei would be clueless with a girl. Fate is gonna hand them a girl. I know it."

Dom snorted. "You're an evil man."

"Lucas is the first of us to have a kid. It's like we're all pregnant with that poor woman."

"Warn us when the cravings kick in. I have a jar of pickled eels I've been saving for a special occasion."

Rowe gave him the strangest look before he shook his head, swore, and flopped down in the chair behind his desk. "You need something?"

"Just making sure I wasn't rotated off Elrige because I fucked up." The first thing he did every morning when he woke was to check the online schedule for security agents. Last-minute changes were a common occurrence, and they'd all learned to quickly adapt to support each other.

Rowe leaned forward, folding his hands on his desk. "Only in the way that we've gotten a serious influx of new business calling since your little window stunt started airing on the news and across the internet. I can't hire fast enough to handle all the new clients."

"That's not a horrible problem to have."

Huffing a laugh, Rowe pushed back and lounged in his chair.

"No, not horrible. But I had Andrei rotate you off Elrige for a few days until the media attention dies down. Right now, you're as conspicuous as he is. That doesn't exactly help you do your job. I've got you working some of the self-defense classes and equipment maintenance."

Dom nodded. He wasn't surprised, but he'd wanted to check that all was cool. Last year he'd been pulled off the active duty roster due to an injury while trying to recover a client. It had taken him months to get back into the field. Now any scheduled time in the office rather than with a client left him feeling twitchy and restless.

With a final wave to his boss, Dom continued to stroll down the hall to the IT room that housed Quinn Lake, Jennifer Eccleston—aka Gidget—and the recently added Cole McCord. Rowe had knocked down one of the walls in that office and extended the space so that all three specialists could work in there. They claimed that they worked best in the same area. Dom wasn't sure he agreed. It seemed like they spent a lot of time arguing with each other in techno gibberish only they understood.

Poking his head in, he found Quinn behind his desk, glaring at his screen through black-rimmed glasses. His dark hair was sticking up slightly, as if he'd been running his fingers through it. Quinn muttered something to himself and then followed it up with a clatter of lightning keystrokes. It seemed too early for him to be tackling a major problem, but then the IT team kept some strange hours along with the security agents.

"Problem with a case?" Dom asked as he stepped into the room.

Quinn jumped in his chair and swore. "Geez, Dom! Make some noise next time." He straightened his glasses and relaxed in his chair again. "No, I'm helping Gidget set up some more servers in Switzerland, and I'm having trouble getting responses from the techs over there because all of Europe takes five freaking weeks of summer vacation! How is anyone supposed to get anything done?"

Dropping onto the sofa across from Quinn's desk, Dom sipped his coffee to hide his smile from the other man. Quinn was so easily flustered. He was also a workaholic, but that had been easing since he'd started dating Shane. Quinn was suddenly finding it easier to step away from work at the end of the day if it meant heading straight into the arms of his man.

"Royce already been through?" Dom asked. He hadn't seen the security agent downstairs, and it had become part of their routine for them to sit in Quinn's office and chat for a few minutes over coffee before heading to their respective tasks.

"Not that I've seen. He's probably sleeping in. I heard that he's got the overnight shift for the Elrige case tonight." The mention of the movie star had Quinn spinning in his seat to face Dom. "So? What's the deal? Is he cool or a total dick?"

"Really?" Dom dropped his head back and cackled. "You're going to fanboy over Trent? We've guarded other celebrities before."

"Yeah, but no one as big as Trent Elrige. I love his movies! *The Second Stain. The Red-Headed League. Silver Blaze.* He's awesome. I'm just afraid that he's a total asshole."

"You can rest easy, Q-Man. Trent's a pretty cool guy. Maybe a little lonely, when you consider all the people who just want to use him for his money or fame."

A slow grin spread across Quinn's lips. "Does this mean someone has finally tempted you away from that guy you've been chasing the past eight months? Ready to give up?"

"Not a chance," Dom said firmly. "Trent's a great guy, but he's not my type."

Quinn laughed. "I thought your type was sexy and willing."

Dom just shrugged. Maybe he had slept around a lot over the past several years, but that changed the minute he met Abe. He couldn't get the man out of his head. "People change. Maybe my type is now sexy and stubborn." *Really fucking stubborn.*

"Good luck with stubborn," a low voice drawled from the open doorway. They both looked up to see Hollis Banner standing there with his hands shoved in his pockets and his mouth twisted in a smirk. "But it makes for fun times when it comes to convincing a guy to see your way of things."

Dom snickered, getting over his surprise at seeing the private investigator at Ward Security. He popped by on occasion to talk to Rowe, Noah, and Andrei. Or when he wanted to "borrow" Ward's IT team to dig into something. Considering that he was standing in Quinn's doorway, Dom was willing to guess it was the latter.

"I'm telling Ian you said that," Dom teased, earning a growl from Hollis. Ian Pierce was close friends with Rowe and probably just as stubborn as his friends. But he was also one of the best chefs in the entire city, so everyone tried to stay on his good side. Of course, Hollis undoubtedly had his sneaky ways since he was engaged to Ian.

Quinn stretched in his seat, trying to see around Hollis's large frame.

"Easy, Quinn. Shane didn't come with me. He's on another job."

Quinn slumped in his chair, glancing back at the email he had open. The poor guy had it bad for his boyfriend, not that Dom could blame him. Shane was a nice guy, cared a great deal for Quinn, and wasn't bad to look at. Of course, Dom had to wonder how nice he would stay if he found out that he was trying to get into his daddy's pants.

"But I was hoping that you could take a look at something for a friend of mine. Maybe run it through one of your fancy databases," Hollis continued.

"I figured you wanted something. Who's the friend?" Quinn asked.

"Detective Martin for CPD," Hollis said. "We worked together a little. She's good. Smart. Fair. But she found something that's got her stumped."

"Sure. Whatcha got?"

Hollis pulled his phone out of his pocket and tapped on it for a couple of seconds before shoving it back into his pocket. "Just emailed the image over to you. It was taken on the side of Carrington Jewelers downtown. They have some kind of show or display coming in with jeweled crocodile handbags, so they're understandably skittish already."

An email popped up on Quinn's screen and he quickly opened it. Clicking on the attachment, the large monitor was filled with the image of a red brick wall. Written in chalk about a foot tall were four distinct images.

Dom was relieved he'd put his mug of coffee down on the little table beside the sofa because he would have likely dropped the hot coffee into his lap. The chalk characters...he'd not seen them in more than a decade. Not since he'd run from his brother.

A cold sweat broke out across his body, and his heart slammed against his chest. *Fuck*. His brother was in town. His fucking psycho brother was in town. Or his father, but he doubted that the old man was still alive. His brother was enough. Every fiber of his being screamed for him to run. To run as fast as he could. *Don't look back. Don't think. Just run.*

By sheer willpower, Dom remained seated on the couch and slowed his heart. He needed to figure out a plan.

It wasn't hard for him to decipher the message. The cipher might not have been a part of his life for several years, but he never forgot it. Judging by the message, his brother was claiming the jewelry store as his next target.

"Dude, that's creepy as hell," Quinn said on an exhale. He leaned close to the screen as if that would make the four little men divulge their secrets.

"Have you seen anything like it?" Hollis asked, oblivious to Dom's rising panic. "It's nearly six feet off the ground, so it's not likely a kid drew it."

"It's weird." Quinn sat up straight, frowning at the image. "Maybe a new gang tag."

"CPD has a comprehensive database of gang tags and this doesn't match anything."

"Well, if this is supposed to be art, the guy is no Banksy," Quinn muttered.

"Who?"

Both Quinn and Dom looked up at Hollis. "Seriously? How does Ian stand to be engaged to you?" Quinn said.

"Banksy is a world-renowned graffiti artist," Dom added.

"This isn't art," Hollis said, glaring at Dom and then Quinn. "I think it might be some kind of coded message."

"That's possible, but the message is too short. Does each image represent an entire word or just a letter?" Quinn shook his head.

Dom cleared his throat and forced his voice to stay even. "When was the picture taken?"

"About three days ago." Hollis leaned over Quinn's shoulder, squinting at the image. "The chalk is clear. Looks kind of fresh. Martin thinks the culprit put it there about four, maybe five days ago."

"I can dig around a little, but tell your friend Martin that she needs to find more if we're going to have a chance at figuring it out."

Dom shoved to his feet, rubbing his hands on his jeans. "I'll leave you guys to it. I've got to get to work," he said, heading as quickly as possible for the door.

As he walked out, he could hear Hollis and Quinn going back and forth, trying to puzzle out the meaning of the message, but they were nowhere close. The cipher was generally a letter replacement code, but he and James had developed a few other images for specific one-word codes. Even though he'd not used the code in more than ten years, he'd been able to read the message in an instant. It simply said: MINE.

∽

James. *James* was in town.

What the fuck was he supposed to do?

The question rattled around in Dom's head endlessly for hours. He'd not seen James since he'd faked his own death and left California. It had been the only way to escape his brother, who'd grown increasingly psychotic over the years. His identical twin brother.

The brother no one knew existed.

No, that was wrong. Rowe knew. When he'd interviewed with Rowe, he'd told him everything when his boss discovered that Dominic Walsh didn't actually exist. He'd told him about the stealing and living on the streets. He'd told him about escaping James and wanting something more for his life before it was too late. Rowe had taken pity on him, given him a shot when he was sure that he didn't deserve one.

Did James know he was still alive? Was that why he was in Cincinnati? The message didn't seem to be directed at him, but then ten years ago, he and James were the only ones who could read their secret language. They hadn't even let their father in on it. Had James come to town with someone else who could read their language?

When they'd been younger, James liked to mark his target with NEXT, like he was taunting the cops. And he got off on eluding the police and child protective services and even other gangs trying to run them off their turf. James wanted the world to know that he was smarter than all of them. Better than them.

Dom went along. Telling himself it was just a game. It was just stuff and they needed to eat. No one was really getting hurt.

Until it stopped being a game and someone got hurt.

His fingers clenched around the gun he was taking apart and he closed his eyes. It took everything to shove back the memory, to bury it down into the darkest depths of his brain. He didn't want to remember it or the ensuing fight with James.

He'd gotten out. Built a good life.

Opening his eyes again, he loosened his fingers and stared down at the gun. He was just supposed to be checking the weaponry and inventory. A mind-numbing job, but they all took turns doing it. Dom usually tried to sweet-talk his way out of it, but today he welcomed the tedious monotony. He couldn't have concentrated on teaching a self-defense class.

Soft footsteps were his only warning before Royce Karras strolled into the room wearing the standard black cargo pants and black polo shirt with the Ward Security logo. They all wore that or something similar on the job unless they were told to appear in a suit and blend.

"Some hero's reward," Royce muttered, jerking his chin at the inventory sheet resting on the edge of the table.

"I'll take it," Dom said, smirking at his friend. "Dealing with screaming fans and pushy reporters gets old fast."

"Thanks."

There was a wealth of sarcasm and derision in that single word, but that was Royce. A man of few words but they carried a shit-ton of meaning when he bothered to speak at all.

"How's Marc?"

Royce's dark expression faded at the mere mention of his boyfriend, and his smirk turned into something closer to a smile. "Begging me to get him an introduction to Elrige."

"Him too?" Dom chuckled. Marc Foster was one of the most successful art gallery owners in Cincinnati. Hell, he had several successful galleries around the world. He was also a damn good artist, though few people had seen his work. Just some friends. And since Royce considered Dom a good friend, he'd been invited to Marc's house and seen many of the paintings Marc had done of Royce. "I thought he knew a bunch of celebrities. How can he need your help?"

"Apparently their paths have not crossed. He claims he's got the perfect piece for Elrige."

"Yeah, and isn't *Silver Blaze* one of Marc's favorite movies?" Dom teased.

"You're not helping."

Dom just chuckled as he resumed cleaning and putting together the Glock in his hands. Royce worked around him, checking out his gun for the evening and the necessary ammo.

The silence was comfortable and easy, but Royce's presence reminded Dom that they both had less-than-pristine pasts, though Royce didn't realize it. Royce had been born into a New York mob family and then worked as an enforcer for a loan shark. Sure, it wasn't the same, but Royce chose to leave that life and start fresh...before it came back to threaten everything.

"Royce...can I ask you a personal question?"

The other man stopped and raised a dark eyebrow at him. "I've never known you to ask permission before. This must be serious."

Dom rolled his eyes and then returned them to the gun in his hands. "Did you ever worry about your past coming back to fuck up your life?"

"You mean like how my uncle nearly killed my mom and almost cost me Marc?" Royce asked, his voice wry.

"Or some variation of that."

Royce chuckled softly. He put the gun he'd been checking on the worktable and leaned his forearms on the top. "I did for a time when I first moved to the area and then when I got the job with Ward, but after a while, I forgot about him. I just concentrated on the job and Marc. The bastard caught me off guard when he struck."

"Now that you know, what would you have done differently?"

Royce watched him for several seconds, his eyes narrowed, weighing him. He could almost hear the wheels turning in Royce's brain as the man tried to figure out the reason for Dom's questions. A part of him wanted to tell Royce, to come clean to all of them, but he was ashamed of his past. He couldn't risk losing them.

"Nothing," Royce said firmly.

"What? What do you mean? You just said your mom almost died, and you could have lost Marc. Why would you not do anything if you could have?"

"Anything I could have done differently would mean possibly missing out on the friends I have here at Ward. It would mean not having Marc in my life. There isn't anything that would convince me to walk away from those two things. My mom is safe, and my uncle is out of my life."

Dom grunted. It had all worked out for Royce, and now he was happily involved with a man who loved him. But was he willing to risk his life—or even Abe's—where his brother was concerned? Last time he'd seen James, he was sure that his brother had gone insane. The guilt over leaving him out there to wreak havoc had nearly taken him down—but James was still his brother and like it or not, they'd had a tight bond during those early years when their father had used them to trick marks.

How was he supposed to protect his friends from James? The only thing he could even think of was packing a bag and disappearing completely. But he loved his life. He didn't want to leave and start all over again. But if it meant keeping people safe...

"Don't run."

Dom's head jerked up at Royce's hard voice.

"Don't run," he repeated in the same unyielding tone. "I don't know what's going on with you, but I can almost hear that thought racing through your brain." He reached out and poked Dom's temple. "You've got a good life here and people who will help you."

He grunted again with a nod. If he opened his mouth, things were going to come spilling out, and he wasn't ready for that. He wasn't sure he ever would be.

A soft sigh slipped from Royce and he picked up his gun. He carefully shoved it into the holster at his side. "Even if your problems turn out to be worse than mine, I'm not going anywhere. You were there when shit went sideways for me. And you were there for Sven when he lost Geoffrey. Your friends aren't going anywhere."

"Thanks, Royce."

Clapping his hand on Dom's shoulder, Royce smirked. "Don't

miss a chance at happiness because you're worrying about what could be. Not what is. If shit hits the fan, we can handle it."

Dom nodded and watched his friend leave.

Was Royce right?

There was little doubt in Dom's mind that his brother was in town. He might have taught others their secret code, but just the arrogance of the message screamed James.

But even if James wrote the message, it wasn't necessarily directed at him. No, if James was sending him a message, it would have been far more direct. And threatening.

If the message wasn't directed at him, then there was a very good chance that James had no idea that he was in Cincinnati or even alive. He was worrying over nothing. And potentially wasting his shot at happiness with Abe. *That* he couldn't accept.

Taking a deep breath, Dom felt some of the weight fall off his shoulders. The pressure on his chest eased, and the jitteriness in his legs finally lessened. He'd be careful. Keep his head down. James would never know he existed, and he'd focus on winning Abe over.

CHAPTER FOUR

"Do me a favor, and don't leave me alone with a blatherskite." Abe lifted an eyebrow as they walked down Race Street to where they were meeting Trent Elrige for dinner between takes. The street had been roped off and large chunks of Washington Park had been cordoned off by the film crew that had been shooting in front of the massive, red brick façade of Cincinnati Music Hall that afternoon. Crowds still milled around the edges, people hoping for glimpses of the actors and actresses. Besides Trent, there were three other big names in this production and apparently, they were all in Cincinnati now for a particular scene, so the place bustled with activity.

"You're expecting that on a movie set?"

"You know what it means?" Dom skirted a couple of people wearing walkie-talkie headsets.

"Are you assuming I don't?" Abe snorted and pointed to his head. "Think there's nothing going on up here? That I'm just a man who works with his hands?"

"I would give anything to know how you work with your hands." Dom gave an exaggerated shudder and nearly ran into a frantic woman carrying a couple of tall coffees. She shot him a glare and took off. Dom laughed softly, but it didn't hold the usual merriment. They walked a few more feet before Dom knocked him gently with his shoulder. "What was it you were saying about your hands?"

Abe shook his head and smiled. He was so screwed. "I suppose I can show you how I carve wood, but really, how exciting is that?"

"And now *you're* assuming I wouldn't watch you," Dom growled at him. "Be nice or I'll absquatulate."

He groaned. "Someone needs to take away your Word a Day calendar."

Dom snickered.

The banter felt good. Abe had noticed something was up with Dom the second he'd climbed inside his car, and he much preferred this over that unnatural quiet he'd been earlier. On the drive, the urge to put his hand on Dom's thigh and squeeze for comfort had been so hard to resist, he'd had to curl his hand into a fist on his lap.

This wasn't good. Not good at all. He was getting attached, and it didn't feel like he was keeping Dom in the friend zone, where he wanted him. Any more and he was looking to get his heart broken.

Not for the first time, Abe wished he was the type to find casual sex easy and fun, because he was fast reaching a point where he wanted...no, *needed*...to know what Dom's skin felt like. How he smelled and tasted. He glanced at him, loving the way his auburn hair shone in the plethora of lights filling the area.

He should have said no to this outing, but turning down a chance to be on a real movie set, a chance to meet Trent Elrige, would have been crazy.

Oh, who the fuck was he kidding? He just wanted to be with Dom.

"There's Trent now," Dom said, grabbing his attention as he picked up speed and waved.

The Clooney lookalike came toward them and his easy smile at Dom made Abe feel a little something he was *not* familiar with. He wouldn't call it jealousy exactly—more like discomfort at the way his eyes sparkled when he looked at the bodyguard.

When that gaze turned to him, then locked on, Abe slowed his walk. Why the hell was the very famous Trent Elrige staring at him so hard? Did he have a smudge on his face or what? When they reached him, Trent nodded at Dom like they were having some sort of telepathic conversation. He waggled his brows.

"This who you chose over me the other night?" he asked when they stopped in front of him. The thin, hipster assistant next to Trent gasped, then bit his lip. Trent rolled his eyes. "Oh can it, Earl, you know what I meant."

"Who's with you today?" Dom asked, shaking the hand Trent held out. "Garrett or Royce?"

"Nobody. You threw the stalker through a window, remember?"

Dom's body went stiff. His frame seemed to puff up a bit in indignation. "You have no security from Ward now?" His gaze latched on to the bruiser standing next to a picnic table outside a trailer.

Trent aimed his thumb back over his shoulder at the man. "I just sent Royce on his way. My usual guy is over his flu and back on the job. He should be enough with the threat removed." He frowned. "You're being rude not introducing me to your boyfriend."

"Oh, I'm not—" Abe started.

"This is Abe Stephens and no, he's not my boyfriend, but that's not from lack of trying."

"Nice to meet you, Abe Stephens," Trent said, holding out his hand.

Abe shook it, noticing he had a lot of callouses. He remembered reading something about the actor paying a lot of extra money for insurance because he climbed as a hobby. He had an iron grip, too.

"So, you don't think Dom here is pretty enough to date?" The wry twist of Trent's lips let Abe know he was messing with Dom. And it worked.

"Pretty? What the fuck?" Dom scowled.

And like that, Abe's tension eased. He liked this guy. "Oh, he's plenty pretty, just not my type."

"And that is?" Trent asked.

"Respectful of his elders."

"We are having a big conversation later," Dom growled under his breath. He held his hands out in front of his chest like he was measuring something. "Big."

Trent cracked up and waved them toward a picnic table. "Come and eat. I ordered ahead—got several things because I didn't know what you guys like."

"You didn't have to do that," Dom said.

Trent shrugged. "Gotta eat and I only have an hour tonight. And I only got that because the director is pissed about something or another. This one usually is whenever his wife can't come on the shoots. If you've seen her, you'll get it." He paused as he settled on the bench. "Or maybe not with you two."

Dom stared at Abe but didn't speak, and Abe realized he wouldn't give away any of Abe's personal information. His heart warmed and he stared back until Dom's mouth went slightly slack.

"Whew," Trent muttered. "You guys better sit down before you catch my trailer on fire. Not dating? Really?"

Abe briefly closed his eyes, then sat across from the actor. He needed to watch himself, or he was going to hurt Dom for real. He focused on the spread on the table, impressed. Sandwiches, subs, salads—and none looked like the kind he made himself at home. These had specialty meats, cheeses, and veggies. Several bright lights had the entire area lit up so much, it was like daytime.

"It's nothing fancy," Trent said. "Things like this are easier to serve when you don't know what time you'll have each day. If you're adventurous, try this one." He pointed to one of the thicker subs. "My assistant found that spicy mustard on our last shoot in Pennsylvania. Has a kick, but a way of bringing out flavors of everything around it."

"You a foodie, Trent?" Dom reached for one of those subs.

So did Abe. He had a thing for good mustards.

"I dabble some, but I eat on the run a lot and with the workouts they've had me doing for this movie, I'm wallowing in protein. Who ever heard of a bulked-up vampire?"

"Not wallowing in blood then, eh?"

Trent flashed them both a quick grin. "Well, I do like my steaks rare."

Bulked out was an understatement. He wasn't as tall as Abe and Dom, but his layers of muscle dwarfed them both.

Abe enjoyed the dinner, surprised he felt no nerves around the easygoing actor. Trent really was like one of the guys, and he had a feeling they'd be friends if he lived nearby.

A woman with sleek black hair and red eyes wrapped in a short, silk robe walked over, her gaze locked on the spread rather than the table's occupants.

"Damn, Trent. I'm jealous."

Abe blinked and stared hard at the woman. It was only when she spoke that he realized that he was looking at Kate Jones, one of the highest paid actresses in Hollywood. But then, she was hard to recognize without her trademark blonde hair and bright blue eyes.

"I do have pretty amazing dinner companions," Trent quipped.

"No offense, gentlemen, but I was eyeing the food. If I have to eat one more salad, I'm gonna murder for real."

Grinning, Trent grabbed an untouched sandwich and pulled off a thick slice of roast beef. He rolled it into a little tube and handed it off to the woman, who consumed it like she was starving.

"There you go, my little carnivore. Just a few more days of shooting and you can binge-eat like the rest of the world," Trent teased.

"You're evil," she said with a little moan. Her eyes finally caught on Trent's companions, and Abe swore he could see a blush under her heavy makeup. "I'm so sorry to disturb your dinner."

"No problem," Abe murmured.

"Kate, these are my friends, Dominic Walsh and Abe Stephens. Guys, the lovely and hungry Kate Jones."

She reached across the table and shook Abe's hand, but paused when she took Dom's hand. "You're the one from the window. You saved Trent's life."

Dom gave a little shake of his head. "It was just a little saving."

Trent made a scoffing noise, but Kate pressed on. "There's a casting agent going frantic around here. I think she's dying to cast you in something after seeing that video of you."

To Abe's shock, Dom went pale at the mention of the casting agent. "Please don't tell her you've seen me. Hollywood is definitely not my thing," he quickly said.

Kate stared at Dom in surprise for a moment and then nodded before turning her attention to Trent. "Sorry about interrupting your dinner. And just a heads up, I think we're going to start soon."

"Wife?" Trent asked.

"That's what it sounds like," Kate added in a low voice. She gave Dom and Abe a last smile and waved at them before walking over to an area that looked set up for hair and makeup.

"She's interesting," Dom ventured when they were alone again.

Trent nodded. "Kate's great. This is our third movie together, and she's so easy to work with."

When people started hustling around them, Trent sighed and wiped his mouth with a napkin. "I've enjoyed this a lot. Maybe you two can hit the town with me once we wrap."

Dom chuckled. "Sure. I know a few fun bars. Like to dance, Elrige?"

"I do, but I rarely do it in public. My lack of rhythm makes me look like a T-Rex doing the pee-pee dance."

Dom snorted. "Thanks for that visual."

Trent was quiet for a few moments as he stared hard at Abe. "I'm about to step over a boundary here, but I have some experience and I can tell you do, too."

His serious tone made the hair on Abe's neck stand up. "I do. Married my high school sweetheart who turned out to be not so sweet."

The nod and smile on Trent's face let him know the man got it more than he wanted to say. There was a twist of longing he understood. He wondered if he was bisexual, too. Wondered what that was like for someone like him. A lot of younger actors were coming out, but Trent looked around forty. He bet it was harder for those who'd been on the big screen so long.

Of course, he could have been reading what he wanted into the situation.

Trent cleared his throat and leaned over the table. "I've met a lot of people in this job. Been all over the world and seen a lot of couples. Met several with age differences larger than yours." Something faint flitted through his expression, something a lot like sadness or loneliness. "Finding someone you really click with is rare. I'm of the opinion you grab on to something like that and hang on."

Startled by his frankness, Abe couldn't help but frown.

"I know. I'm being nosy."

"Hella nosy," Dom muttered.

The awkward conversation was thankfully thwarted by a frantic young man in a headset running up to their table. "You need to get to makeup now. Derek is on the warpath. Seems wifey number four was spotted somewhere not so…wifely."

"You're such a gossip, Fred," Trent muttered, sounding truly annoyed. "I'm sure Derek appreciates you spreading that around so casually." He waved his hand at Dom and Abe. "I have guests."

The guy looked at Dom and gasped. "You're the one from the video!" He dug his phone out of his pocket and clicked on the screen a few times, then held it out.

Abe read the title.

Who's the Hot Ginger with Trent Elrige?

Dom's startled gaze met Abe's as the video played, and something in his expression sent alarm through Abe. He tore his gaze away to watch Dom kick a guy through a window in a crazy impressive move.

Trent grabbed the phone and held it up to his assistant. "Who the fuck took this?"

The poor guy paled. "I think it was the person who was going to interview you."

Trent turned back to Abe and Dom. "I'm sorry about this. People will do anything for a buck these days, and my life is never left private. It's the price of this job. But I'm sorry you got dragged into it, Dom."

"I should have been more diligent," Dom said, half under his breath.

"You were a little busy saving my life and showing off some sweet kickboxing moves. Did you see my expression in that video? I had no idea I'd hired Van Damme." He laughed and waved off Fred, who seemed happy to escape. "I've got to run, but the part we're filming in this city should be wrapped up soon. It's going to be longer than I thought, but I'll call when it's done. Want to take me out and show me your fair city, gentlemen?"

Dom stood and held out his hand. "Will do."

Abe shook his hand, too, still surprised how easy and fun the whole experience had been. As he and Dom headed back for their car, he was surprised by Dom's somewhat grim mood. He remained quiet outside of asking Abe to come to his house for a beer. He had a feeling it was for a drink *and* a talk.

Dom seemed particularly vigilant as he parked in his driveway and led Abe into his house, his head swinging right and left. He also alarmed his security system fast, his hands shaking faintly, like he vibrated with some kind of nervous energy.

Prickles rushed along Abe's skin because he got the distinct feeling Dom was protecting him and if that was the case, then something had him spooked.

"Beer?" Dom asked as he swept past him.

"Sure," Abe murmured, following him into the kitchen, which Dom had remodeled with dark gray cabinets and black appliances. He stared hard until those pretty green eyes met his over the open refrigerator door. He tried to read what was wrong because he had the strongest feeling it had nothing to do with the personal situation between them. "You okay, Dominic?"

His shoulders deflated for a moment before he gave Abe one of the sweetest smiles he'd seen on that face. "Yeah, I'm fine. I have some things on my mind. Tell you what, with that slight cool front that moved in tonight, why don't we enjoy these outside?" Dom asked as he shut the door, two bottles in his hand. "I have something really special to show you."

Abe rolled his eyes at the slight return of innuendo as he let himself onto Dom's back deck. Dom had told him before that the house had actually been built in the early 1900s, and he'd kept all the original white brick, including this archway that led to the modern deck. He smiled when he spotted chaise lounge chairs at the back of the property past some trees.

Dom followed as he walked down the stairs to the grass. Abe looked around with appreciation at the midsized backyard. "You have a lot of nice, old trees back here," Abe murmured, stroking his hand down the bark of a sycamore. "This one is massive. Does the bark turn white in winter?"

"It does. These offer great shade in the summer, but keep walking underneath to the chaises."

When they reached that spot in the yard, Dom pointed up.

Abe lifted his gaze and sucked in a breath at the clear spot of sky with hundreds of twinkling stars.

"I have no idea why this particular patch of sky is this flawless, why none of the pollution or city lights seem to affect it, but it was a nice surprise after I bought the place. I come out here at night all the time. It's my favorite spot to relax."

"I wondered why these lounge chairs were set so far from your house, but now I get it." Abe took a beer and settled in one of the chairs, his large chest dwarfing it. "Join me?" He waved his hand at the other chaise.

Dom stretched out, and they were silent for a few moments.

Abe took a deep breath of the air, which was still warm but

carried a faint coolness now that felt good in his lungs. He relaxed and let himself soak in the stars.

"Abe?"

"Yeah?"

"You're frustrating me to death."

"I know," Abe answered, his voice hushed. He rolled his head on the chaise to stare at the man who had taken up so much space in his head. Moonlight sharpened the lighter strands in his auburn hair and shone on his face. The need in his gaze did what it always did to Abe —made his breath catch and his heart pound.

Dom looked away, taking a swig of his beer and looking back up at the stars. "I don't understand, to tell you the truth. I don't know what to ask. What to say. I can tell you want me."

"I do."

"And?" He sat up and swung his legs to the side of the chaise to face Abe. "It can't be all about the age thing, Abe. What has you so spooked? Can't you tell there's something big here? Is it because I'm male?"

"Are you asking if I have a problem being attracted to a man? Because that's not it. I've known I was bisexual since middle school."

"Oh." He looked down at his beer.

Fuck. He needed to just open his mouth because he was hurting the man when all he wanted was to not get hurt himself. Patricia did a number on his heart and it may have been years ago, but that kind of soul-deep pain left a mark, one he wasn't ready to share yet. And the other reason was humiliating, but Dom deserved more.

Abe took another deep breath and this one didn't feel as good, because his stomach started to churn. "I've never been with a man, Dom. Never even kissed one."

That made Dom's head whip up. "What? At all? I mean, I suspected your experience was limited, but nothing?"

"You heard me," Abe said quietly, closing his fingers tight around the cool beer bottle. "I have absolutely no idea what I'm doing when it comes to men." He sat up. "I met Patricia when I was young, and it was so hot with us, I never looked at anyone else. After she left me, I hooked up a few times, but that was always with women. Each time, I was left feeling empty…and I don't know. I just didn't like how I felt afterward. I figured out casual sex wasn't for me."

"I've never said I was interested in just a hookup."

"No, but you like to have a good time, and you like it with variety. You told me that yourself the first weekend we met."

"That was true then," Dom said with a little groan. "But things change. People change. I really like you."

Abe sighed. "Dom, I really like you, too and love having you as a friend. Hell, I don't have a lot of friends outside of my son and Quinn. I don't want to fuck this up. So not only do I have trouble having casual sex, and especially with someone I like so much, I'm…" He cleared his throat and chuckled. "I have no idea what the fuck to do."

Dom looked…flummoxed. Abe didn't blame him.

"I know, crazy, huh?" Abe set his beer down on the ground and ran both hands through his hair. "I'm forty-nine years old, and I feel like a bumbling teenage virgin."

"But you…" Dom released a nervous laugh. "You split up with her twenty years ago. You're saying in all that time, you never even tried anything with a man?"

"Not even a kiss. I've had sex with women, but it wasn't a priority. Some of my hesitance was due to how I let things go with my ex, but some was because of the financial crash in 2008. I spent years focused on digging myself out of a hole. Sex just wasn't something I felt I needed to focus on. When I got the itch, I went with what I knew."

"Why?"

"I love the expression on your face." Abe laughed. "Women are great, Dom. But you're attracted to only men, so you can't see how I resisted, right?"

"Pretty much."

He stared, his palms sweaty again because this had suddenly

become so important. Dom wasn't some hookup to experiment with, and he needed to be honest. Needed to make sure Dom didn't think that was what he was doing here. "Ever avoid doing something because you don't know how to do it?"

"You have a dick, Abe. You know what feels good." Dom stood.

"Yeah, I do," he breathed as he got out of the chair. This was it. Maybe Dom wouldn't end up being the permanent partner he was interested in, but he was tired of fighting this.

Anticipation and nerves buzzed inside every inch of his body, and he suddenly didn't care about the difference in their ages or whether Dom's body was eons better than his own. He just wanted his fucking hands on him. He pulled Dom close, noting that the man had started to slightly pant already as Dom's eyes roamed his face.

"Fucking finally," Dom muttered as Abe took his mouth. He also grabbed the back of Abe's neck with one hand and held him so tight, Abe couldn't have pulled away even if he wanted to.

And he certainly did *not* want to.

His dick grew rock hard with the first touch of Dom's lips, and all worries about knowledge or fumbling instantly evaporated because all he could think about was how Dom felt. How he tasted. His lips, softer than Abe had expected, felt so damn good on his and he ran his tongue along the seam between them. Dom opened immediately to let him in, but he was no passive participant on this ride. He brought his tongue out to play, and the sensual glide of it made Abe groan in the back of his throat.

That noise seemed to do something to Dom, because he gasped and let go of Abe's neck to grab his hips, yanking him close.

His blood rushed so fast through his veins, he felt dizzy. Need clawed at him and he cupped the sides of Dom's face and deepened the kiss, greedy for every taste he could find in the man's mouth. The whiskers were a new sensation, prickly around his mouth, and he loved it. As much as he loved the hard body pressing to his. Dom's cock felt like a pipe against him, and he couldn't stop himself from shifting just enough to rub his own against it.

Dom gasped into his mouth again. "Yes," he breathed, digging his fingers into Abe's hips, grinding into him.

He'd only meant to kiss him—to see if the spark he'd felt from the beginning translated through actual touch. But this? This was *insane*. He hadn't felt desire like this in longer than he could remember. Had possibly never felt anything like this—and his relationship with his wife had been passionate. But he didn't want to think about her. He and Dominic had been dancing around this elephant for months.

He needed to touch his skin and didn't think as he ran his hands up under Dom's T-shirt.

With the first touch of skin on skin, Dom lifted his mouth and turned his face so their cheeks were together, panting so hard, his words came out more as puffs of air. "I. Knew. It. Had a feeling."

Abe couldn't talk. He moved his lips down to softly bite Dom's jaw, then brought up one hand to thread his fingers through Dom's hair, pulling him back and baring his neck. He kissed and licked his neck, while he ran his fingertips over Dom's side, exploring muscles and silky skin.

If he'd ever wondered if a man would turn him on fully, he did no more. He was burning up and just touching the smooth, warm flesh of Dom's abdomen made him shake.

"Damn. There's not an ounce of fat on your body." He brought his mouth up to kiss Dom again. "I like your skin, Dominic."

"I like your everything," Dom growled, taking over the kiss with a strong thrust of his tongue.

Abe had never been kissed quite like this, and the power of it went to his head again. When he had to pull back to breathe, he whispered. "You haven't seen my everything."

"I've looked at you enough to know what's under those clothes, and I love everything I've imagined. I also know it won't compare to the real thing." He bit Abe's bottom lip, sucked it into his mouth, then let it go with a tiny pop. Then he wrapped his arms tight around Abe and just held on. He buried his face in Abe's neck. "I can't believe I'm saying this, and I'm positive I've lost my mind, but we need to slow this down."

Shock zipped through him. "You've been pushing for this for months." Dom squeezed him tighter. God, the man felt good against him.

"I know. Now I'm scared. So, we're going to have to take this slow. Fuck, Abe, what if we have sex and you find you hate it? I think maybe...I think maybe I wouldn't handle that so well."

"Yeah, that's not going to happen. Trust me. I'll more than likely embarrass myself with how long I've been holding this in, but I'll like it. I'll like everything."

"Don't worry. We are definitely not done yet." Dom kissed his neck, pulled back and pressed a long, soft kiss to his lips. "Come on, I'll drive you home."

"I'll just grab a cab."

"Nah, I want to take you home and kiss you on your doorstep like a proper date."

Abe held his breath because it felt like he was standing on the edge of a cliff that was so tall, he couldn't see the ground. Was he really going to do this? It wouldn't be permanent—couldn't be—but what if he did ride this out? Enjoy Dom's company as a friend and a lover and maybe...just maybe some of the wild restlessness that had been tearing him up lately would ease.

He threaded his fingers with Dom's and didn't let go as Dom walked them back through the house and grabbed his keys off a hardback book on Russell Square on the table next to his front door. He turned off his security system to reset it.

They walked out onto the front porch and Abe let go when Dom went perfectly still, perfectly stiff. Abe followed his gaze to find something on Dom's front door. Chalk figures had been drawn across the surface.

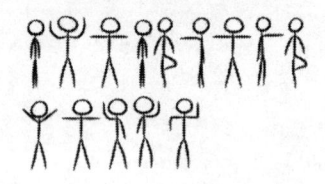

Dom moved behind him to the edge of the front deck, his body coiled with tension and alert as he looked around his front yard and driveway. "Let's get you home, Abe." His voice was so tight, the words came out clipped.

"What the hell?" Abe pulled out his cell to snap a picture, but before he could Dom came back and smeared his hand across the chalk. "Why'd you do that?"

"Neighborhood kids think they're funny." Dom shrugged, but it was anything but casual. "I'll clean it off when I get home."

Dom was lying. And lying wasn't something he did—Abe knew this on a fundamental level he couldn't explain. But he decided to let it go for now. When Dom looked away, he snapped a quick picture with his phone of what remained. He had the strongest feeling that message or whatever it was had nothing to do with kids, because it had Dom spooked.

And a spooked Dom worried him.

CHAPTER FIVE

Lightning streaked across the dark sky, followed by a deep roll of thunder. Dom picked up his pace down the sidewalk, hands fisted at his sides. He wanted to get inside this next club before the rain broke free. The summer air had been thick and humid earlier in the day; then it had cooled before a brisk wind had picked up. A storm was about to dump buckets of water on the city.

Red neon lit the night, shining the name Jubilee. It would make his third club of the night, but he had a feeling that he'd get lucky with this one. Jubilee had opened a little more than a year ago, but the owner refused to pay for a decent security staff. The place had turned into a gun and knife club in a matter of weeks. Fights broke out regularly, and the place had been featured on the news several times due to violence that occurred in or around it.

Dom had popped by one time a few months after it opened, then swore he'd never be back. He liked a place that got a little rowdy, but he didn't want to worry about getting knifed in the back because someone didn't like his shirt.

He might not have seen his brother in years, but he was sure James hadn't changed that much. Jubilee was a good fit for him. The kind of place where he could shoot off his mouth without people taking any real notice of it. Where he could push people around and be a big shot, if that was what he wanted that night.

Stepping inside, Dom gave a curt nod to the doorman, who barely glanced up from his phone to see Dom as he walked by. Barely aware of his surroundings, he wasn't checking IDs. Dom forced his thoughts away from the guy and stepped into the main bar. Music blared out from speakers spread around the dimly lit club. There was a little more light at the bar, where a pair of bartenders were furiously working to keep up with drink orders as customers stood nearly three-deep at the scarred oak.

A dance floor occupied the middle of the club, and it was packed with people sweating and gyrating in the intensely hot building. Dom could already feel his T-shirt starting to stick to his back as sweat ran down his spine. Not only was the owner hiring shit security, but he also wasn't willing to put in adequate air conditioning to keep up with the number of bodies filling the small space.

Fuck it. He had to find James. His brother knew he was alive and where he was living. If he didn't face him, James could quickly infiltrate the rest of his life. Dom didn't want to risk the lives of his friends. He also didn't want to risk the truth of his past getting out. Abe couldn't know. Not yet. Preferably not ever, but definitely not yet.

Dom glanced over the customers at the bar, but it was easy to see that there was no one there resembling his brother. Frowning, he turned away and edged toward the dance floor. James had liked to dance a bit, mostly when he was completely lit and celebrating a successful job. There was still no sign of him among the people dancing to the throbbing beat of the music. Strobe lights flashed and colored lights swirled in a hypnotic kaleidoscope, but it wasn't enough to distract him from seeking his target.

Rowe had trained them for these kinds of situations, showed them how to stay aware in a dark, crowded place with seemingly endless threats all around them. Of course, Rowe's first bit of advice was to always get the package out of that situation as quickly as possible, but clients regularly refused to live a cloistered life just to make things easy on their bodyguard.

Confident that James wasn't on the dance floor, Dom sidled through the throng of people to the far wall. If he remembered correctly, there were several booths and tables along the back wall of the place and then a pool table in the back room. He edged along the rough brick wall, trying to see around the partiers, when his heart lurched in his chest.

James.

It was like looking in a mirror. They were nearly identical. Only the scar running down the left side of Dom's face marked their difference. He hadn't been on an official job when it happened. The explosion at the house where local Instagram celebrity Geoffrey Ralse had been held had caught him by surprise, resulting in several scars running down the left side of his body. His first thought when he'd realized the scars were a permanent part of his appearance was relief. For the first time in his life, he knew he was different from his brother. Piercings and tattoos could be mimicked, but the scars made him unique.

More than ten years had passed since he'd last seen his twin brother, and the man still looked just like him. They had the same haircut and the same muscular build. How? He didn't want to think about other personality similarities. Growing up, they'd liked the same foods, same music...and the same men.

Raising a shaking hand to his face, Dom roughly rubbed his eyes while leaning back against the brick wall. Thicker shadows cloaked him from the view of the table. He needed to get his head together. There was no doubt now. James was in Cincinnati, and he wasn't alone.

He looked at the circular table again and did a quick count. His father wasn't there, but again, he was sure the old man was probably gone. He'd been old when he'd fathered them. Besides James, there were five other men. None of them were familiar, he noted with a feeling of relief. None of Dom's acquaintances had mistaken James for him, but that was only a matter of time the longer James remained in the area. Dom knew a lot of people, both former clients and friends. He couldn't risk James impersonating him.

The other five men were muscular bruisers with matching cold, angry expressions as they leaned close over the table, talking. This wasn't a relaxed bullshitting session where they conversed about a sporting event. They were planning something.

Fuck, six against one were horrible odds. He didn't stand a chance if they caught sight of him. He should have brought backup. But who the hell was he going to ask to drag into this mess?

Abe.

The man's handsome face came to mind instantly at that question. It both caused Dom's heart to race and a chill to break out across his arms. He wanted to go to Abe with his problem, to share it with him and get his advice on what he should do next. But the idea of telling him about James, about everything from his life in California, was terrifying. The guy had just barely survived a horrible marriage. He had a perfect life now with his son and his woodworking business. Abe Stephens did not need the shitstorm that was crashing down on Dom's life.

Swearing under his breath at himself, Dom looked back at the table where James and the other men continued to talk. It was hard to look away from his brother. Now that he'd gotten over his initial shock, it was becoming easier to see little differences between them. His brother's expression was colder, harder. The lines around his mouth and eyes were deeper, making his face appear harsher than his own.

Watching James was like watching a ghost of himself, a talking image of what he would have been if he'd stayed in California and continued to steal and work cons with his brother. How much innocent blood would have been on his hands by now? How many lives would they have destroyed together?

He had to get out of there. He needed to go home, regroup, and come up with a smarter plan. James had a fucking crew now that he ran with. A low, bitter laugh rose up. James had needed to bring on five guys to replace him.

Regardless, he had to get out of there before someone noticed him. Tracking down James and telling him to get the fuck out of Cincinnati had to be a one-on-one conversation. He couldn't win against James the way the odds were currently stacked.

Heading back the way he'd come, Dom carefully made it around the dance floor, keeping his head down. Being tall with red hair made him too damn easy to spot in a crowd. Progress slowed as he reached the bar. The number of people ordering drinks had increased, and no one was willing to let him ease his way through for fear that he was going to steal his place in line to get alcohol. He was sorely tempted to just shove his way through, but that was the last thing he wanted. Glancing to his right, he could see the front door not more than a few hundred feet away.

A heavy arm landed on his right shoulder from behind while a forearm came across his chest, pulling him in tight to another tall, large frame.

"Babe, I said I'd get the drinks on my way back to the table," someone said in a laughing tone in his left ear.

Dom froze. His first instinct was to throw the arm off, but the stranger's words proved that he thought Dom was James.

"I've got it. Go back to the table," he replied in what he hoped was a tone that matched James's.

"Or you can come back to the bathroom with me now. They're not too crowded." The stranger's other hand slipped across Dom's side, along his stomach, heading down toward his crotch. "I'll get on my knees for you." Disgust crawled along Dom's skin. His brain panicked. What the fuck was he supposed to say?

He couldn't take it. Roughly throwing off the man's arms, Dom stepped away from the guy, pushing other people out of the way. "Get off me and go back to the table."

Dom's heart gave a little flutter when he finally got a good look at the other man. They were about the same height, and he had rugged good looks with dark hair and deep brown eyes that would have called to him not so long ago. Yeah, he and his brother definitely had a type. But he'd found Abe, and that shit didn't matter anymore.

A confused and hurt expression twisted up the man's features, but it only lasted a second. Surprised pushed his eyes wide and parted his lips. He spoke, but Dom couldn't hear his voice over the loud music. He read his lips, though.

You're not James.

Dom smirked. "Still wanna suck my dick?"

The man's face turned bright red and his mouth snapped shut. Like he'd let this asshole anywhere near his dick.

Dom grabbed a handful of the man's shirt and shoved him backward through the crowd, toward the bathroom, down a small hall to the left of the bar. He knew the guy was going willingly. They were the same height and build. There was no way he could move the bastard if he didn't want to go.

Inside the brightly lit and smelly bathroom, Dom slammed the guy's back against the light gray wall. The fucker just smiled at him. Of course, he smiled. He knew that Dom was outnumbered badly. Dom hadn't seen this guy at the table. He must have been in the bathroom when he'd spotted James. That meant James had a crew of six instead of five. Seven against one were still shitty odds. He had to get the hell out of there before anyone came looking for this asshole.

"Why is James in Cincinnati?" Dom snarled.

"John," the man said with sickening pleasure. Dom shivered at the name. He'd given up that name when he "died." One of the few people to ever use it was James. "He's looking forward to talking to you."

Dom ignored his comments. Tightening his fists in his shirt, Dom pulled him forward a little before slamming him back against the wall. The few people already in the bathroom zipped up their flies and hurried out of the restroom. Even with the lax security, he figured that he had only a minute or two before someone came in to investigate the disturbance. Or worse, before James or one of his other crew members came looking for this dickbag.

"What the fuck does he want?"

The guy just stood there, taking Dom's anger, his smile growing on his face with each furious word. "We came to town for a job, but we're staying for you. He's not leaving without you."

"Fuck you. And fuck him. I'm not going anywhere with him. Tell him to get the hell out of Cincy. Go back to California."

Dom released James's lover and took a step toward the door, but a hard hand clamped down on his right wrist, holding him in place. He didn't think. He just reacted. Left hand fisted, Dom swung around and plowed it right into the man's jaw. He instantly released Dom's wrist and swung his own left. Dom blocked the blow with his forearm. The impact rattled bones and he gritted his teeth. The bastard was solid.

He couldn't let this stretch. The guy was just trying to keep him there, so he could be discovered. Time to fight dirty. Dom almost smirked. Couldn't get much dirtier than a bar bathroom fight.

Smashing his left forearm across the prick's jaw, he grabbed his hair with both hands and pulled his head down while bringing his knee up. Cartilage and bone crunched. The man shouted, this deep voice echoing off the walls and porcelain. Keeping him bent over, Dom fisted his hand in the would-be attacker's shirt. He stepped backward and propelled him into the partially closed metal door of an open stall, then threw him into the toilet. There was a clatter of noise and shouting along with the sound of flushing. Probably caught his hand on the handle as he attempted to straighten.

Dom didn't wait around for the guy to climb out of the stall and take another swing at him. Darting for the door, Dom hurried back into the club. Music hammered his eardrums, and he blinked against the dark room broken by the flashing lights. People moved around but he couldn't make out faces yet. Didn't matter. He shoved his way through the crowd, tunneling through the people still gathered in front of the bar. There was no sign of a bouncer or other staff beyond the bartenders slinging drinks behind the bar. No sign of James yet.

Sliding past the last of the crowd, Dom rushed to the door and outside. Rain poured down in nearly blinding sheets of cool water. Streams rushed down the sidewalk and rushed through the debris-clogged gutters. He paused on the sidewalk for only a second, running his hand through his hair, slicking it back. Rain soaked into his clothes in a matter of seconds, plastering them to his frame.

He didn't feel anything beyond relief to be out of there without catching his brother's notice. He needed to get home. Regroup. Plan. There was no facing his brother while his crew was around. He had to catch James while he was alone if he was going to have any hope of reasoning with him. Of course, that hope might have died the moment he beat the shit out of the asshole who'd groped him while he was trying to get past the bar.

As the door started to close behind him, he heard a shout rise up above the music, angry and ruthless. He had to get the fuck out of there.

CHAPTER SIX

He should have canceled the date.

Dom tightened his fingers on his steering wheel as he drove to Abe's the next night. He'd wanted this for so long, he couldn't bring himself to do it. He'd always been a little pushy about the things he wanted. It came from a childhood where he never had anything he hadn't taken for himself. Gifts had been few and far between, and even those had usually come with a price.

Especially when they came from his father or brother.

Their father had already been in his fifties when they'd been born, and he'd lived life hard. A grifter who'd been thrilled with identical twins because he could use them. Love hadn't been a part of the picture, and by the time Dom had run, his father had already been withering away. Didn't matter, he and James had grown up on the streets, so he had little attachment.

And their father had taught them plenty in the early years, forcing them to go along with his plans, which included nobody knowing they were twins. Two identical faces—one public one. And one public name.

Fuck, so many years had passed, and he'd grown complacent.

Comfortable. There was no way in hell he was going to let James ruin this life he'd built.

Dom took a meandering, long route to Abe's that night. Was he being overly cautious? Probably, but dragging James into Abe's world was the very last thing he wanted.

By the time he parked in Abe's driveway and knocked on the door, his adrenaline, worry, and anger had swirled into this volatile mix, and he knew he definitely shouldn't have come. *Damn.* A first, real date with the man of his dreams and he was ready to take off someone's head.

Then Abe opened the door and some of his tension eased at the sight of the gorgeous man. Some. Lust ramped it up as he took in the heather gray Henley that accented his muscular arms and wide chest, the low slung, loose and faded jeans that hugged his slimmer lower half, especially his ass when he turned to shut the door.

Dom leaned against the entryway wall, unable to take his eyes off the man. Abe turned and must have read the desire on Dom's face, because he narrowed his eyes and stepped close. Dom shut his eyes, inhaling the fresh, showered scent and that aftershave that drove him a little crazy.

"I needed this," he whispered.

"Bad day?" Abe stepped even closer, the heat of his body seeping in to warm Dom's. Despite the summer temperature, he'd been cold since seeing his brother the night before.

"The worst." He opened his eyes to find Abe's gaze on his mouth and the punch of desire that hit his gut made him suck in a breath. He lifted his hands slowly, running them up Abe's forearms. He'd bunched the sleeves up to his elbows, and he had soft hair on his arms that felt good against his palms. "You're hairier than me."

"Is that a good or bad thing?" Abe still watched his mouth.

"Oh, good. So, so good." He wrapped his fingers around thick biceps and pulled Abe into his body, sliding a leg between his. His heat, his scent, wrapped Dom in a cocoon of masculinity that went to his head. "You have this same hair on your chest?"

"It's curlier," Abe murmured as he took Dom's hands and ran them up under the hem of his shirt.

Lovely warm skin and crinkly hair met his palms. Dom groaned and closed his eyes again. He dropped the top of his forehead onto Abe's shoulder and explored his belly and chest under the shirt. He did have crisp, wavier hair on both sections. He slid his hands around to the smooth skin of his back. "Abe?"

"Yeah," he said on a faint moan.

"You feel good." He nuzzled into his neck. "You smell good." He opened his mouth over Abe's pulse, licked, then pulled back. "You taste good."

"Fuck, Dominic." Abe's voice went guttural and he brought Dom's face up to capture his mouth in a kiss. He nipped Dom's lower lip, then lightly sucked it into his mouth, making it slippery and wet. Dom opened his mouth and Abe dipped his tongue in, running it over his lips again, mixing them together.

It was so fucking hot, he started to shake.

He speared his fingers into the curls on Abe's head and thrust his tongue into Abe's mouth. He tasted even better there, and before he could register the electricity tearing through him, Abe tugged him as close as possible and surprised the hell out of him when he grabbed one of Dom's ass cheeks and kneaded with strong fingers.

Dom gasped against his mouth, groaning again when Abe licked into his own over and over, their tongues meeting in a hot, wicked dance that they both started to mimic with their hips.

He'd meant to take tonight slow. He hadn't meant to ravage the guy before he got fully into his house. Fuck, he wondered what things Abe would like. Hoped he was verse because Dom wanted to sink into his body just as much as he wanted to feel the man inside him. That thought made him shudder, which caused Abe to pull back and press their foreheads together as they panted. He ran his hands up Dom's back to his neck and cupped it. He held Dom's head still as he nuzzled into his cheek, then kissed him—this time softly, with his mouth closed.

"Damn," Abe murmured.

Dom registered a noise then. An oven timer beeping. "I'm surprised you heard that. My heart is beating so hard, it's all I hear other than your breaths."

"Heard what?" Abe asked. "I heard something?"

Snorting, Dom pulled him in for a hug, took his scent deep into his lungs, and let go. "I guess you cooked for me?"

"Shit! The oven!" Abe shook his head, pulled away, and he hurried through his living room into the kitchen.

Smiling and completely tickled that the man had cooked for him, Dom slowly followed, taking in the house he'd only been inside a couple of times. It looked bigger on the outside—like a reverse Tardis—with a compact living room and kitchen. A bar-style black table and with two bench seats and two chairs separated the areas. He knew there was a dining room off to the side Abe never used. He had buttery soft brown leather furniture facing a fireplace with a television mounted on the wall above in the living room. The only other piece of art was an antique sports sign that Abe had told him belonged to his father.

It looked like a family kind of home. Warm. Welcoming. Like the man.

Dom leaned on the white counter of the small island and watched Abe pull out a pan of potatoes. "Those look perfect."

"Little crisper than I wanted, but they'll work. You like pulled pork?"

"Oh, hell yeah. So that's the heavenly smell." He sniffed, then grinned. "And if I'm not mistaken, there's something sweet in the air?"

The faint red on the back of Abe's neck as he turned back to the oven made Dom want to do a dorky dance of happiness.

"I've noticed you have quite the sweet tooth. It's nothing special. A banana nut bread Shane is nuts about."

"I'm touched. I had no idea you could cook. I have a few tricks up my sleeve there, too."

"I'm not that much of a cook, actually. I have about ten recipes I got the hang of over the years, and I stick with what I'm good at. Lots of different kinds of sandwiches mostly. You learn what you can when you end up a single parent." He chuckled and lifted the lid off a crock pot.

The spicy barbecue that filled the air made his stomach growl, and he realized he hadn't eaten anything since a bagel that morning. His damn brother had his mind all jacked up. But James was the last thing he wanted to think about. Watching Abe putter around his small kitchen filled Dom with a feeling he didn't recognize. A sort of peace and comfort that duked it out with lust. He knew he wasn't looking at the man as a father figure in any fashion. Wasn't looking for a replacement for the shit stain that had been his dad.

He just really, really liked Abe, and he didn't give a damn if he was turning fifty soon.

And yeah, he'd wheedled that information out of Quinn without giving himself away today. He'd had to pat himself on the back for that one.

"Can I help with anything?" he asked as Abe got out plates and forks.

"Nope." He paused. "I'd planned to take you out somewhere nice tonight."

"This is nicer than anything we would have gotten out."

He grinned and Dom wanted to nuzzle back into his beard. Abe handed him a plate. "You haven't even tasted the food yet, so save that thought."

"I meant I'd rather be here with you than go out." He picked up Abe's plate too and carried it to the table.

"I thought we'd go out afterward. You can show me someplace you like."

He didn't want to risk running into his brother. Not tonight. He grabbed two bottles of water out of Abe's refrigerator and sat at the table. "Let's eat and then maybe we'll Netflix and chill."

"Trying to trip up the old man?"

Dom looked around. "What old man?" He winked. "Netflix and chill means—"

"I know exactly what it means." Abe leaned over the table until he was a breath away from Dom's mouth. "And I have Netflix."

"Shit," Dom breathed, his body igniting back to full burn so fast, it made him dizzy. "For the record, please don't think I'm eating so fast because I don't enjoy the food. I love it."

"Again, you haven't tasted it yet."

"Doesn't matter. You and me?" He waggled a finger between them. "We have a date with that couch in less than fifteen minutes."

Abe sat fast and they both dug in.

∽

Dom insisted on helping him clean the kitchen, and it took all Abe's concentration to not attack the guy. He wanted to lift him up on the counter and—

"That's it," Dom announced. "I can't handle the way you keep looking at me." He threw the dishtowel he'd been using and backed Abe into a wall this time. He braced both hands on either side of his shoulders and stared hard at him. "We're doing this at a slow pace. I mean it."

"Stop being so fucking bossy and come here." Abe grabbed him and yanked him in for another kiss that rocked his world. The man kissed like he wanted to devour Abe, like he could pull air from Abe's lungs to survive on that alone. He had a naughty tongue normally—Abe never knew what was going to come out of his mouth—but it was also playful and so damn sensual when he slid it into Abe's mouth. He wanted that tongue all over his body.

They kissed until his lips became sensitive, to where every rasp of Dom's lips sent nerves tingling like he was being zapped with tiny bursts of electricity.

Dom pulled back and he kept going until his back hit the island. "Take off your shirt."

Abe didn't even hesitate. He was too far gone to worry about his forty-nine-year-old body at this point. If Dom didn't like him as he was, if he didn't want to do this again, then Abe would take this one shot to see him, to touch him, and he'd love it. He took a step forward and pulled off his Henley and stood there, letting Dom look. "Yours too."

"In a minute," Dom breathed as he leaned back against the island and leisurely ran that hot gaze over Abe.

It took all his control to stand still because he wanted to maul Dom. There wasn't another word to describe what he wanted to do. Grab him, throw him against the wall or on the couch and just...take him apart. Feel all that searing skin against his. Rub his cock against that taut body...

Dom grinned in that oh-so-wicked fashion of his and crooked a finger. "Come here."

But Abe had a better idea. He grabbed him and pressed him back into the wall. Dom didn't wait for him to take the final step closer before his hands were on Abe's chest and his fingers were combing through his chest hair. He ran one palm down Abe's belly, which didn't have the bumps and ridges of muscle that Dom's had. But he couldn't discount the complete desire he saw in those green eyes and the very hard dick showing in his jeans.

Abe slowly reached out and ran one finger down that hard ridge, and the back of Dom's head thunked on the wall. "If I come in my pants, no comments about the age thing. I'm thirty-two damn years old and you have me so hot, I'm about to be humiliated for life."

"Oh yeah?" He popped the top button and unzipped Dom's jeans. He didn't push them down—just left them open. "Spiderman? Really?"

"I didn't think you'd be seeing my boxers tonight, or I would have worn the Batman ones. They're way hotter." Dom smirked.

That expression was so fucking sexy, and Abe wanted to mess with it, so he reached inside the waist of Dom's comic-covered underwear. Dom sucked in a loud breath when he wrapped his hand around his cock. "Did you think I'd have my hand on your dick today, Dom?"

"No. I hoped." He panted and let out a hoarse noise when Abe tightened his fingers. "I hoped every damn day since I met you." He ran his hands over Abe's chest. Up, then down and each time, he played with the hair. "I kept seeing hints of this peeking out of the openings of your shirts or a glimpse when your T-shirt was loose, and it's been driving me nuts for eight fucking months."

Abe glanced down, hardly able to compute anything Dom was saying because he loved the feel of that long cock in his hand. It felt like his, smooth skin over rigid muscle, the pound of blood pulsing under the surface. But it also didn't feel like his. It was silkier and hotter, and he wanted to explore every inch of it with his hands and his mouth. He ran his thumb over the crown and felt the bit of slick beaded at the top. When Dom shuddered, he felt like puffing out his chest. He was doing this to Dom. *Him.* "What was driving you nuts?" he finally whispered.

"The hair on your chest. It's darker than what's on your head and in your beard, and I was dying to see just how dark and how far it went down. I like that it disappears into your jeans. So damn hot." He stroked Abe's stomach, then stopped and took a long, shaky breath. "I think we're going to have to slow this down."

Regret laced every word, but it was obvious he meant what he said.

"Why?" Abe asked, tightening his fingers and chuckling at the way Dom gasped and thrust up into his hand.

"Because I really like you, and I know how you feel about dating. I don't want to just hook up with you, so I want to go slower, too. So you'll know it's real to me."

"Feels pretty damn real to me." He frowned. "I've heard the stories, Dom. You don't do slow."

His eyes opened and the green shimmered in the low light of the lamp behind Abe. "That's just it. Nothing about this feels anything like what I've done before." He curled his fingers in Abe's chest hair again. "This matters, Abe. Really matters. You like the way it feels to kiss me? Touch me?"

"I like it a lot more than I expected, and I expected to love it."

Dom's chuckle was so low and throaty, Abe's dick jerked in his jeans and he winced and glanced down at it.

"Well, I've been with a lot of men. Enough to know the kind of excitement I'm feeling right here with you is more important than a hookup."

Abe stared at him, his heart still slamming against his chest and his cock still hoping for more action. He stared until he clued in that this was important to Dom. He meant every word. He reluctantly uncurled his fingers, but he used both hands to tug the waistband of those silly boxers out so he could look inside. He grinned when Dom groaned.

"That's cheating."

"I just wanted to see what I have to look forward to. You going to teach me what you can do with that thing?"

This time, his eyes squeezed shut and he purposely slammed his head back against the wall. "I'm an idiot. Never mind. Ignore everything I just said and slide your hand back in there."

"Nope," Abe said, kissing the corner of his mouth as he refastened Dom's jeans. "You're right. I want us to both be ready for that first time."

"But there will be a first time, right?" Dom's eyes shot open and narrowed on him. His hair was stuck up all over the place, and he had beard burn darkening his cheeks and jaw—his pale skin flushed red down his neck.

So. Damn. Hot.

"There will definitely be a first time. And probably a second. And a third." He stepped back.

"God, I'm an idiot," Dom repeated. "You find us a movie—not on Netflix, dammit. Something with lots of explosions. I'm going to run out to my car. I got us a nice baby bourbon. No telling on me that it's from New York."

Abe just flat-out liked him. "Bourbon sounds good." He watched Dom hurry out his front door and he walked over to his freezer, opened it, and stuck his head inside. Holy shit, he was on fire. He'd had passion in his life, but this was unreal. Kissing Dom was like taking a shot of a good, one hundred percent bourbon. Smooth and a little sweet with a kick that left a man warm, horny, and fired up for more.

When he felt sufficiently cool, he got out a packet of microwave popcorn. Popcorn and bourbon? He was up for trying something new. Or...something else new.

He had absolutely no doubts that he was going to love any and every kind of sex he was going to have with Dominic Walsh.

When the popcorn was done, he poured it into a bowl while watching his front door. He wasn't sure what sent alarm skittering down his back, but within moments, he was out the front door and the sight of Dom running from around the back of his house had him rushing out to his driveway to meet him.

The absolute fury and fear on Dom's face made his food turn into a lump in his stomach. "What's going on?"

"Fuck, Abe. I'm so sorry. I have to go. Now. But I'll be back with paint to take care of that tomorrow, okay?"

"Take care of what?" Confused and worried, he grabbed Dom's arm to stop him from getting into his car. "Paint? What's wrong? You look...scared."

Dom pointed and Abe followed to see some black letters on his white garage door. He let go of Dom and walked close, realizing as he did that they weren't letters, but stick figures in different poses.

"These are just like the ones you said neighborhood kids did on your door." He crossed his arms and stared at Dom, taking in how pale he looked in the light of the streetlamps. "Talk to me. This is obviously not kids—not ones who followed you to my neighborhood. What do these figures mean?"

"I don't...I can't." He shut his eyes and scrubbed both hands over his face. "I'm not sure what this means, but I have to leave so I can find out. I'm sorry to cut our evening short, and I'm sorry about the door. I'll fix it tomorrow."

"I don't give a rat's ass about the damn door, Dom. This is bad. I can tell. You said you wanted more than a hookup, and that means communication!"

Dom's lips tightened, and a flash of agony flashed over his expression.

"Dom?" Abe stepped toward him.

But Dom jumped into his car and shut the door. He mouthed, *I'm sorry* through the window before peeling out of Abe's driveway.

Abe stared after him for a few moments, then looked back and forth down the dark street. He saw no movement and he didn't feel eyes on him, so he was sure he was alone. He walked to the garage door and saw that someone had used actual paint to make the figures. This time, Dom couldn't wipe them off.

Because it was obvious this was some kind of evidence, he walked inside to get his cell phone. This time, Abe would have pictures of the entire message.

CHAPTER SEVEN

The familiar scents drifting through the air at the Norfolk Pub the next afternoon didn't settle the uneasiness swirling through Abe's chest. He had a standing lunch date with Shane and he usually looked forward to it, but today, he had too much on his mind.

Just a few days ago, he'd decided to tell his son about Dom, but now he found himself reconsidering. And it didn't have anything to do with the fact that Shane's boyfriend had joined them. Quinn couldn't have been a better fit for their little family, and it was obvious he was a permanent part of Shane's life. Abe's decision had more to do with the way Dom had acted the night before. His concern sat like a weight on his shoulders, and he had a feeling he shouldn't talk about what was going on yet. Not the relationship or the stick figures that had been gone when he left his house that afternoon. Dom must have returned at dawn to paint over them.

Luckily, Abe had taken plenty of pictures.

The scent of toasted bread, pastrami, and roast beef filled the restaurant, and all the tables and blue booths were full. The place was known for its Binham Blue Cheese and specialty mustard. The owner had come from England and brought a taste of his home with him.

His son loved the food, too, so he'd scored a reservation early today.

Quinn's face lit up when he spotted Abe and he waved him to their table, which was already set with the colorful clay pottery made in one of the seaside towns in Britain. Various images of sailboats and sea creatures peppered the walls, and a white sail was stretched near the ceiling over the bar. When he'd first come here, he'd expected seafood, which he loved, but he'd been so pleasantly surprised by the cured meats. And the special was always a delightful surprise.

A place was already set for him; Shane knew him well.

Abe walked over to the table, smiling at his son as he looked up at him. Happiness lit Shane's brown eyes—mirrors of his own. In addition, Shane had inherited his curly hair. He'd gotten his slimmer build from his mother. He wasn't as slim as his boyfriend, though, who was cute with his dark hair and black-framed glasses. Seeing these two with each other was the highlight of any day they got together because there was a magic there he'd hoped his son would find. Something real and lasting.

"Dad." Shane stood and hugged him.

Abe held his son and smiled. He loved that they were so close now. Shane had been angry with him for years because of Patricia and the way he'd indulged her. Far as he was concerned, he deserved the anger. She'd walked all over him at times because she knew just how important family was to him. He'd wanted to keep her in Shane's life, so he'd given in on so many things. Hadn't mattered in the long run—she'd still walked out on them both.

"Hey, Abe." Quinn smiled up at him, then pointed to the glass of iced tea. "I hope unsweetened is good, because I ordered when Shane was outside on the phone. He told me you always get the special, no matter what it is."

"I do, and unsweetened is fine. It's good to see you."

"You too."

Their food arrived as he settled into his chair—like the waiter had just been watching for his arrival. This being his third time for sandwiches this week, he'd have to cut the bread for the rest of it. He'd never get down to the weight he'd enjoyed in his younger years, but staying in shape was important. Especially now that he had a hot boyfriend.

Wait, was Dom a *boyfriend*?

The thought made him feel both silly and giddy at the same time.

"You look good, Dad. Happy." Shane picked up his fork and jabbed a piece of lettuce out of his salad. He paused with it on the way to his mouth. "You look really happy. Work going well?"

"It is." Abe took a bite and closed his eyes at the hit of hot mustard and pastrami. "Oh yeah, that's the ticket," he breathed. He took another bite and moaned. He opened his eyes at the silence across the table.

Shane looked at his boyfriend. "Dad and food."

"It's like porn," Quinn said with a cheeky grin.

"Hey now, no mentioning porn in the same breath as my dad." Shane shuddered and dug into his salad.

Quinn snorted. "Shane, I hate to break it you, but your father is a genuine hottie." Quinn said it so matter-of-factly, he made Abe blink. "So the work is going well, you said? Did you get more orders for those custom window frames?"

"Pretty sure everyone on my street has put in an order now, so I'm booked."

"Chairs, too?" Shane asked.

He nodded and wiped his mouth with a napkin. "A restaurant downtown put in an order for one of their rooms. Surprised me because the chairs aren't cheap."

"Wow," Shane breathed. "At this rate, you'll have to hire someone."

"Hire someone to do my hand-carved specialty woodwork?" Abe shook his head. "Nah, I'd like my Stephens Chairs to stay made by a Stephens. Let me know if you want to learn." He waggled his brows.

"But if it stays this good, I'll be able to do it full time. I'll need a bigger workshop, though."

"Oh!" Quinn said, excitement lighting up his blue eyes. "The last time I was at your house, I noticed how full your garage is getting, so I looked into a few places." He paused and chewed on his bottom lip. "Hope that's okay?"

"Of course it is. Thank you."

He beamed at Abe. "So there are some places down near North Bend Road for rent that wouldn't be too far from your house. Have you looked at those? They have reasonable prices and no noise ordinances." Quinn picked up a baguette and tore off a hunk to dip into his soup. "I remember you said you had to start late in the morning on some of the projects because of your neighbor's baby."

"I've actually had trouble knowing when it's okay to run the saws. Babies sleep on different schedules than we do. And another of my neighbors is elderly and she sleeps midafternoon. I know because she brought me cookies and asked if I could run the saws in the mornings."

"So, damned if you do and damned if you don't."

Abe nodded. "How's your mom doing, Quinn?"

The young man's smile wavered a little bit and Shane's hand slipped under the table, likely to squeeze Quinn's leg as he'd seen him do a dozen times in the past. "She's okay. There are good days and bad days. The doctor made a little tweak to her meds recently, and it seems like the good days are starting to outnumber the bad again, which is always a plus."

"Definitely," Abe said with a nod.

His expression suddenly perked up again and he smiled broadly at Abe. "She asked about you when we visited last week."

Abe's head jerked back in surprise. Quinn's mother had been involved in a horrible car accident when Quinn was in college and suffered brain damage from which she never fully recovered. Quinn had explained that her memory had been bad after the accident and was growing worse with age. Abe had met Charlotte only the one time and it was over a month ago.

"That's amazing."

"Yeah, she was wondering if my handsome father with the killer smile was going to come visit her again," Shane said with a leer. He stole a hunk of bread off Quinn's plate and dipped it into his own soup.

"Hey now," Quinn teased, smacking Shane's hand. "You had your own and scarfed it down."

"Yours always tastes better anyway." Shane winked.

Abe laughed, completely pleased with Quinn, so glad he felt comfortable enough to check into something like that for Abe. He really was a part of the family already. Which meant...he needed to be here for what Abe was about to say. He might not be ready to talk about Dom, but it was time his son knew about him. The voices around him became a drone of noise and he took a deep breath. Then another. This was harder than he thought.

He wasn't in any way ashamed of who he was; it was just telling his *kid*.

"I wanted to talk to you two about something today." He cleared his throat. "I'm seeing someone."

Shane's grin was a flash of white teeth in the dark scruff on his chin. Scruff that held no hints of gray yet—but he was young. Abe ignored the ironic voice in his head saying Dom was the same age.

"Oh yeah?" Shane asked. "It's about time. Where did you meet her and when do we get to meet her?"

"Well, that's the thing." He paused and wiped his suddenly sweaty palms on the cloth napkin in his lap. He fiddled with it until Shane cleared his throat.

He looked up to find real concern on his son's face.

"It's not a...her," he blurted.

A heartbeat passed, then another, before Shane started to laugh and held his hand, palm up, to Quinn. Quinn shook his head and pulled out his wallet and handed twenty bucks to Shane.

"Wait, you two bet? Is this not a surprise?"

Shane placed his elbows on the table and leaned over it. "No, Dad, it's not. You look at guys. You've always looked. I just wondered if you'd ever take the chance and act on it."

"And I didn't think you would," Quinn piped in.

Abe pointed a finger at Quinn. "We'll address how you think I'm a wuss at a later date, Quinn." He waved the finger at both of them. "So, it's been obvious to you both?"

Quinn nodded. "He's right. You *look*." He smiled. "So...bisexual?"

"For as long as I can remember being attracted to people. My first real crush was a boy. But then, I just fell in love early and I'm a one wom—person man." He shook his head, then picked up his tea to wet his dry throat, trying to ignore that his hand was still shaking a little. "And here I was so worried about telling you this."

"Why?" Shane slung his arm around Quinn. "It's not like I'd have reason to judge that one. Not that anyone should."

"No, but it's different when it's a parent, and you've believed something about him your entire life. I've always wanted to talk to you about it but wasn't sure how to approach it."

"I wish you had. You can talk to me about anything." He gave Abe a pointed look. "So who is he? And I'll repeat, when do we get to meet him?" He sat back again and pulled Quinn close, his hand cupping Quinn's shoulder possessively, his thumb stroking him.

He'd changed so much. Was so deeply in love.

And Quinn still sometimes looked at Shane like he couldn't believe how he'd lucked out. They were both so damn lucky.

Abe wanted that for himself now that his son was settled and happy.

"This is still too new for meeting the family. I'm still new at... everything." *Shit.* That had just popped out. He really, really wished he hadn't said that and hoped his *child* would think the heat on his neck had to do with the sun streaming into the restaurant windows.

"You know, I changed my mind. Maybe we can't talk about everything," Shane mused, his face showing some color, too.

Quinn rolled his eyes. "Abe, if you need pointers, I'll help."

"No!" He held up his hands, a little horrified at the thought of hearing any pointers Quinn might have learned with his son. "I'm good. I'm great."

Both Quinn and Shane lost it then. By the time Shane was wiping his eyes with his napkin, Quinn was asking for a doggy bag.

"I have to get back to my office," he said as he leaned over and kissed Shane's cheek.

Shane turned, grabbed his face and gave him a loud smooch on the lips. "Now you're as red as we are." He waggled his brows. "I like it."

"You're incorrigible," Quinn grouched, but one corner of his mouth rose. He looked at Abe. "Don't think *you* got out of the trip discussion just because you stole the limelight with your announcement, Abe."

"Really guys, I have too much on my plate for a trip right now."

"But it's your fiftieth birthday," Shane argued.

"And now he has someone he may want to spend it with." Quinn kissed Shane one more time, waved at Abe, then wove his way around the tables to leave.

Shane watched him the entire way with a small smile.

"I'm glad you're happy, Shane," Abe said, his voice low. "I'm glad you didn't let what your mother did color how you see relationships. That you took a chance. Quinn is wonderful."

"He's the best. I'm the lucky one." He tried to hold back a giddy grin and lost. "I talked him into moving in with me."

"That's good news! He stays there most of the time now, doesn't he?"

"Yeah." Shane pulled out his wallet when the waiter arrived with their bill. "But he hadn't brought over all his things. Far as I'm concerned we were already living together, but this makes me happy.

He's the one, Dad." He held up a hand when Abe grabbed his wallet. "I got this one. It's a celebration of you finally coming out."

"Feels a little anticlimactic."

"Maybe because it's not a new revelation for you or for me. It's still a really big deal that you told us." Shane leaned closer. "I'm happy for you. And happy you met someone who is putting that spark back in your eyes. You deserve it."

Abe couldn't help but feel like Shane wouldn't handle the "who" part of this as well. "I don't know that it's anything permanent. Right now, we're just getting to know each other, really." He held his breath. "He makes me a little crazy, to tell you the truth."

"Good! That's exactly what you need." Shane got the tab back and he signed it, then stood. "Let's do this place again next week. I'm getting what Quinn got today. That tomato soup is amazing."

Abe thought he'd been stealing food to mess with Quinn, so he chuckled as they left the restaurant. The summer heat was back after the short break the night before. He hugged his son good-bye, then headed to his truck. He was on Glenway Avenue when he realized the same car had been behind him when he'd driven to lunch earlier.

The hair on the back of his neck rose. Thinking he was imaging things, Abe spotted a comic shop with a T-shirt of Spiderman in the window. That could be fun to wear the next time Dom came over. Hoping they had it in his size, he pulled behind the store and parked. As he walked around and into the front of the shop, he noticed the car slowing as if the person driving was looking at him. He couldn't see through the tinted windows well enough to know what the person looked like—only that their face was turned his direction.

The car suddenly lurched, tires screeching as it took off down Glenway.

Abe stood staring after it for a long time because that gaze had carried enough malevolence to turn all the food he ate into a burning lump in his gut.

CHAPTER EIGHT

Abe gripped the piece of sandpaper tight in his fist and sent it back and forth over the outside of his favorite window frame design. It held a tree that started thick at the bottom, growing from the bottom center, with naked branches filling the top—naked to show the flow of branches and to let light in through the window.

As a kid, he'd drawn trees often. He liked the way the branches snaked out to diverge into smaller ones and how all the lines in a drawing followed comforting parallels. There'd been a massive tree in his backyard as a child and he'd played underneath, sheltered from the hot sun. Later, he'd climbed it, especially after he and his father had built a treehouse.

He wished he had more trees in his yard now, but he'd gotten this house for a steal when a friend had to transfer jobs fast. He'd just managed to pull himself out of the financial mess he'd been in after the crash, but it had been a hard-won battle. Now, he had the house and a small nest egg for safety.

Safety had always been his priority. That and family.

He'd never understood how Patricia could throw that aside—how she could have walked out on Shane especially. God, he'd been the sweetest kid ever with his big brown eyes and dark curls. A bubbly baby who belly-laughed at everything. Abe had loved him instantly and been sad that his own parents had never gotten over his young fatherhood. They'd been so angry and had just started really being a part of Shane's life when they'd been killed in a car accident. Shane had been only two years old.

For the longest time, it had been Abe, Patricia, and Shane against the world. Then she'd grown tired of the financial struggle. She'd always been kind of selfish, but her true colors had come shining through the more bitter she'd grown.

He moved the sandpaper over the trunk, pushing memories of his ex-wife away and moving on to Dom. He flashed back to that kiss under the stars and his hand paused. Fuck, that kiss had been nice. Just like the ones they'd had here the night before.

Though nice didn't really describe those. Holy fuck, had that been something. He'd never felt such excitement and...heat.

It had been so long since Abe had felt anything like that and even now, a kind of giddiness filled him at the thought of doing more with the man. It had been all he could do not to cart Dom the few steps to his couch last night. What would it feel like to lie on top of him and feel all that heady strength and smooth, smooth skin underneath him? He'd felt the scars the night before, but they hadn't detracted from Dom's beauty at all. Those scars made him feel more real, more human, than the almost godlike Adonis he appeared to be most of the time. He wanted to spend time tracing his fingers along them, learning them. Learning every inch of the man.

He wanted to go to Dom's now, but showing up three nights in a row would look pretty damn needy.

He paused again. Worry intruded on his happy memories of their moments together. He'd never seen Dom so upset, so on the edge of panic. The guy always had a smile on his lips, that look of happy-go-lucky ease and contentment. The way he'd left Abe's house last night was wrong.

And what about the car following him? Pretty coincidental, considering the stick figure drawings showing up everywhere.

A return of the restlessness that had been driving him crazy lately crept through him.

Was all this a midlife crisis? The agitation, the paranoia...Dom?

He swore and stood to throw the piece of sandpaper, but it wasn't a very satisfactory heave since it only went a couple of feet before hitting the floor. He should throw something larger.

Or just do what he damn well wanted.

Abe stomped through his house to shower the sweat off his body and not long after, he was steering his truck to Dom's. He opened and closed his hands on the steering wheel and by the time he'd gotten to Mount Airy, he'd realized fear was tearing him up. That a genuine feeling of wrongness had been plaguing him since the first drawing. And there'd been something in Dom's expression the night before that told him the messages were not good.

But what could they be? They looked like children's drawings.

He knew the man was a badass fighter with skills in martial arts, but Abe found he wanted to look out for him. To protect him just like he knew Dom would do for him.

He pulled in to the right of Dom's car, turned off his truck, his heart beating like a bass drum in his chest. Maybe this was a bad idea. Dom was a freaking professional bodyguard. The man was trained to handle intense, dangerous situations. What was he hoping to do? He turned the key again, planning to pull back out, but Dom stepped out onto his deck and grinned at him. The absolute mischievous slant to that smile told him that the guy was reading his mind. There was a lot in that smile. Delight and amusement—like he was thrilled Abe had come but knew he was about to flee.

So instead, he took a deep, calming breath. They wouldn't have to do anything he wasn't ready for. He got out of the truck and his cell phone clattered to the concrete. He kneeled to swipe it up and something caught his eye. He gasped when he realized it was another, different set of stick figures.

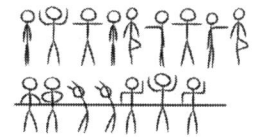

This time, some asshole had keyed them into the side of Dom's beautiful, white Beretta. He aimed his phone at the symbols, hoping Dom couldn't see the flash.

"What are you doing out there?" Dom called out.

He hurriedly pocketed his phone and stood. "You aren't going to like what I'm looking at, Dom."

Dom came down the steps and around his car.

"Jesus Christ!" He strode close and kneeled, his chest heaving. "That sadistic motherfucker."

"Do you know who's doing this?"

Dom just...deflated. His shoulders slumped, his eyes closed, and he put both hands in his hair. Then it was like a switch had been flipped, and he was looking into the dark shadows of the trees surrounding his property, his body alert and tense.

"Dom?"

"We gotta talk, Abe. But we need to do it inside, okay?"

"Anything," he said softly, clasping his hand on Dom's shoulder. "I'm here for anything you need. I'd like to know what's going on. What's upsetting you."

He just nodded, then surprised Abe when he took his hand off his shoulder and threaded their fingers together. He tugged. "Come on. This is going to require a stronger drink than beer."

Abe hated the sound of that.

∽

Dom's mind raced as he led Abe inside. He let go of his hand and walked through the house into the kitchen, where he kept the good booze in one of his upper cabinets. He poured them each a glass of bourbon.

He couldn't tell him everything because it would kill him to see what Abe was starting to feel for him fade out of those beautiful eyes. He stared into them as he handed Abe a glass. They were such a gorgeous shade of brown, warm and caring. They could fill with passion so fast, it made Dom's head spin. The *man* made his head spin.

He couldn't lose the ground he'd gained—he just couldn't.

"Someday...maybe...I'll tell you a story about a boy who didn't have a lot of choices growing up, but right now, I'm going to tell you part of his story. When he was twenty-two years old, he faked his death."

Abe's face paled.

Dom's lips tightened, his palms sweating so badly he pulled a towel out of the drawer next to the sink. He ran it through his hands, twisting it into a rope. The rush of joy he'd felt when he'd heard Abe's truck pull into his driveway had been so intense; the punch of fury over what his brother had done to his car had his head swimming. He'd just showered and thrown on comfortable shorts and a T-shirt. The past several minutes had been spent trying to talk himself out of sitting outside Abe's house—in case James went back there.

If his brother was at all the same, his cat-and-mouse game would last longer. He wouldn't actually go after Abe until he'd driven his brother mad with worry, forcing him to act.

James got off on psychological torture, but Dom was terrified he'd taken that need to a more horrific level when James had discovered he'd been tricked all these years.

"Dom?" Abe walked up to him and set down his glass on the counter. He pulled Dom tight against him. "You faked your death?"

Dom nodded against him, digging his fingers into the strong muscles of Abe's back, the memory of what he'd had to do still having the power to stab him through the chest. "I deliberately burned down the house where we'd been living. I stole some cremated remains from a funeral home so that some bits of bone would be found, but not enough to run a DNA test. Made it look like a gas explosion so that everything was destroyed. And I ran. Like a fucking coward. I ran and never looked back. I...I just had to get away. There was no other choice."

"Hey," Abe said as he tipped Dom's head up with both palms over his ears. Brown eyes met his, and the concern mixed with lust snapped him out of his anxiety. "We don't have to talk any more about this. You can share the rest with me when you're ready, and I'll be here to listen. What can I do right now? Should we call the cops?"

Dom was quick to shake his head. "No. No cops. I don't want the cops involved in this. At least...not yet."

"Then what if we call Shane? He's a private investigator and has some experience dealing with some strange stuff."

"No, but thanks. You're all I need right now." He turned his face into Abe's neck, brushing his lips against his jaw. "I just want to relax and think for a while. Figure out a plan."

"Then how about I try to take your mind off things?" And with that, he brought his mouth to Dom's.

Dom melted into his touch. Now this was a program he could get behind. Sex would wipe away all memories of his brother because his attraction to Abe seemed to wipe out all thoughts anyway. And now was no different as fire swept through to obliterate everything else. He parted his lips and Abe took the kiss deeper, his tongue scorching a path of fire in Dom's mouth.

He reached up to thread his fingers through those soft curls he was fast becoming obsessed with. The night before, he'd imagined Abe rubbing his curly hair all over his body.

Moaning, Abe ran strong hands down his back and dug his fingers in to clutch Dom as close as possible. His entire front was plastered to Abe, and he felt his hard dick as Abe began to move his hips side to side, rubbing against him.

Dom hadn't put on any underwear and even with his eyes closed, he couldn't stop them rolling back into his head. When Abe groaned and gripped his ass to suddenly grind, he nearly came in his shorts.

He pulled away, gasping air into his tight lungs and wrestling himself under control. "I like your idea," he panted as he turned and pulled Abe out of the kitchen, up the stairs, and into the hall, backing slowly toward his bedroom. He was fucking trembling with excitement, never having felt this hopeful about another man in his life. This kind of lust—it was something else. It raged through his body like a firestorm. The backs of his knees hit the bed and Abe just kept coming, his brown eyes narrowed and so full of intent, Dom shivered.

"You're shaking," Abe murmured, his hand coming up to cup Dom's jaw. "Shouldn't I be the nervous one here?"

"Because you're a man-virgin?"

Abe snorted. "That just sounds so wrong." He softly kissed Dom's lips.

Dom pulled away slightly. "What if you hate this?" His voice was barely above a whisper.

"I won't."

"You don't know that. I don't think I could stand being the man who proves this isn't what you want."

"Dom," Abe growled as he grabbed Dom's hand and placed it over the iron spike filling the front of his jeans. "I'm more turned-on than I've ever been in my life, so you have nothing to worry about except me throwing you to that bed and taking you apart."

"Yes, please." He nearly barked the words.

Abe grinned suddenly and kicked out, effectively swiping Dom off his feet so he fell back onto the bed.

"Well that wasn't very fucking romantic," Dom muttered even as he laughed and wiggled farther up the comforter. He got to the pillows and started to yank off his T-shirt, but Abe stopped him by crawling up his body and dropping his weight on him.

Dom groaned, his mouth opening for the kiss Abe gave him. And holy shit, the man could kiss. He fucked with his tongue, moving it in and out of Dom's mouth, tasting and sucking on Dom's tongue. He nipped Dom's lips, then ran his cheek over the scruff on Dom's face.

The rasp of Abe's beard felt so good on his skin, he held his breath and clutched his sides.

Abe wiggled his hips and Dom opened his legs, wishing he'd taken long enough to get out of his clothes. "Skin," he breathed against Abe's cheek as the man sucked his earlobe into his mouth. "Gah!" he cried out. "This would be better naked."

Abe put his hands on either side of Dom's head, his large frame pushing back and away from Dom. Dom started to complain, although he'd been the one to request the loss of clothes, but his tongue twisted into knots when Abe tugged off his shirt and revealed his wide shoulders and barrel chest. Brown and silver hair curled between and around his nipples and down his belly. Muscles bulged in thick arms. Dom had been privy to the upper-body strength of the man and right now, all he could do was take in the heady masculinity hovering above him. His hips were narrow compared to his upper body, and Dom pushed him farther back.

"I want to see it all. Stand up and show me."

He was glad he'd left the light on because he would have missed the faint flush of red on Abe's neck as he stood and reached for the fly of his jeans. He undid it and pushed them down, revealing leaner hips that flowed down into thighs thick like his arms. He had round, muscled calves and long feet. Dom brought his gaze back up to the gray boxers and couldn't manage to form words enough to ask for their removal. Fuck, he was so excited, he felt like a teenager.

But Abe pushed the underwear down, his dick rearing up and leaving a faint glistening trail on the hair on his belly. His cock was thick, the tip wet, and Dom's mouth watered.

"Am I the only one getting naked? Because I have to say that wouldn't be my first choice." Abe's low words yanked him out of his trance.

Dom scrambled off the bed to take off his own clothes, but his hands seemed to have a mind of their own as he instead ran his palms down Abe's chest and stomach. He stroked fingers over Abe's hips and around to the smooth skin of his back. He stepped close and nipped at Abe's bottom lip. "I love your body."

"Pretty sure I'm going to love yours too, when I get to see it."

Chuckling, Dom stepped back and tugged off his T-shirt, pushed down his shorts, and kicked them off.

Abe groaned. "I knew you were flying free under those damn thin shorts."

"Like them, do you?"

"I like what's under them a lot more. Fuck, Dom, look at you." This time, Abe's hands did the mapping of Dom's body. He started with his shoulders and when he stroked his palms down Dom's arms, he couldn't keep himself from flexing—just a little. He had to bite back a grin when Abe moaned softly and continued his exploration, grazing the backs of his fingers over Dom's abs. "You're like a work of art. Like something I'd see in a museum."

"Shut up," Dom murmured. "I'm just a guy and I'm not the gorgeous one here."

Brown eyes met his. "You make me feel gorgeous."

"I wish you saw what I do when I look at you. What I'm pretty sure Trent saw when he looked at you. Did I tell you that I felt a little jealous and a lot possessive after seeing that?"

"Oh, yeah?"

Abe's fingers drifted back up his chest, across the long scar from the explosion he'd been in during the mission to save Geoffrey Ralse. "Not quite museum quality. More scratch and dent," Dom nervously joked. Was it wrong that he wanted to be perfect for Abe? To be exactly what the man craved.

"Better than museum quality. You're real. And mine."

Abe must have tired of talking then, because he grabbed Dom as he turned and fell back on the bed, bringing Dom over on top of him. "Oh God," he groaned. "I knew that smooth skin of yours would feel good against me."

Lust shot through him so hard, he felt his balls drawing up way too fucking early. Again. Nope, that wasn't happening. He shut his eyes and willed the racing orgasm back. But Abe grabbed his head and started that expert kissing of his. Dom sank into him and opened his mouth. Tongues dueling and sliding—teeth nipping. He was ravenous suddenly and he straddled Abe, spreading his legs and letting that fat cock of Abe's rest against his crease.

Abe froze.

Panting, Dom tore his mouth away and sat up enough to get a good look at the man beneath him. He expected to see hesitation on that gorgeous face, and instead he saw such an intense level of desire, Abe looked like he was ready to blow as well. His breaths were coming fast and hard, and he writhed under Dom in a way that had Dom biting his lip.

"Move like that again," Abe whispered.

Dom placed his hands on Abe's chest and slowly rubbed his ass back against Abe's dick. He rolled his hips. "Is that what you want? Want inside me?"

"Yes. No. I don't know."

He couldn't help the small smile because so far, there was absolutely nothing telling him that Abe wasn't one hundred percent into this. "You'll like it."

"No doubts on that here." Abe thrust up his hips, rubbing the soft tip of his cock over Dom's hole. Back and forth and back and forth until Dom was gritting his teeth.

"I do want inside there at some point, but there's something I really want to do first."

"Anything. I'm yours for anything."

"Lie back."

Dom lifted his leg and rolled onto his back. Air left him in a rush when Abe came with him, rolling on top. "Oh, you feel so good on me like this. Shit."

Abe was too busy nestling his entire body on Dom's, nuzzling his jaw, then his neck. Dom nearly came up off the bed.

"Good spot?" he murmured, his breath hot against Dom's collarbone.

"Yeah. Love attention there."

Abe placed his teeth around Dom's pulse and bit.

"Agh!" Dom cried out, bending his head back to give Abe all the access he could possibly want.

"I love discovering your sweet spots. Got more?"

"Yeah, several. Have fun."

Lips moved down his chest and to his nipples. He bit and licked, then sucked Dom's nipple into his mouth. Dom hissed and bucked up again. Abe chuckled and kept going. As he drew close to one of Dom's other spots, he started to shake. His lower abdomen—he loved to have that kissed, and when Abe reached that spot, he clutched at those soft curls on his head and moaned.

"Oh man," Abe breathed as he nuzzled Dom's bellybutton, and before Dom could utter anything else, Abe had his hand on Dom's cock and his lips in his pubic hair.

Dom's eyes slammed shut and he waited, barely able to breathe. His big hand stroked up and down, fingers tight around his dick.

"Love how silky the skin is here."

"Lemme feel yours."

"In a minute. I'm acquainting myself with all of you. Been thinking about this a long, long time."

"Oh yeah? Since when?"

"That first fucking night you stayed in my house and walked around with your shirt off. Shameless hussy."

"You know it. Still, it took you long enough to come around."

"I'm here now and hopefully, coming soon." He moved down and shocked the hell out of Dom when he kissed his knee and came up. That was when he discovered Dom's other weakness. Abe licked his inner thigh, and the whimper that came out of Dom's throat would have embarrassed him if Abe hadn't bitten down softly in that moment.

"Damn," Abe murmured softly as he gently tugged on Dom's balls. "You're ready to blow. Not yet."

"You're killing me." Dom reached down to grab himself, but Abe's mouth beat him there. He licked the tip of Dom's dick.

"Oh," he breathed like he loved the taste.

Dom figured he only had a few moments to live then. He couldn't get his lungs to work properly, and the effort to hold back his orgasm was making his brain hurt. Right when Abe went to take him farther into his mouth, Dom pulled him off and curled up as he lost the fight. He bowed up off the bed as he shot all over his stomach and chest. Some hit his chin.

When his vision returned, it was to see Abe grinning, his expression more smug than Dom had ever seen it. "I did that to you."

"You did," Dom panted. "I feel like an idiot."

"Don't." His chest puffed out. "I made that happen and I'm proud of it."

"Goof." Dom sat up and grabbed the T-shirt he'd thrown onto the bed. He wiped himself off, tossed the shirt to the floor, and pulled Abe back to him.

"Missed a spot," Abe said as he licked Dom's chin.

And like that, the tingling started up in his body and his dick perked up a little. Knowing it would take more to bring it back to full mast, Dom still moaned when Abe came in for another kiss with the taste of Dom on his tongue. It was time to show this man what he could do with his mouth.

Dom pushed him to his back and slowly explored as he moved down Abe's body. He nuzzled into the hair on Abe's chest. He'd always loved a hairy man. His own body had so little, and what he did have on his legs and arms was sparse and more red than the auburn hair on his head.

He reached that fat cock and nosed below, taking in the scent of Abe, who had obviously showered before coming over, but who also still smelled faintly of sweat and musk and man. He went lower to see if Abe's inner thighs were as sensitive as his and smiled against his skin when Abe quivered. He came back up and didn't give Abe any warning, taking that beautiful cock into his mouth slowly and surely, hollowing his cheeks, and relaxing his throat so it could keep sliding until his lips met his hand at the base.

"Agh!" Abe bellowed, voice deep, before the yell broke off into a hoarse cry as Dom sucked back up. He licked the underside, went down, and swirled his tongue around the base before coming back up to suck him back down again. The whole time, he listened to Abe's noises and when there were good ones, he repeated whatever he was doing until he had turned Abe into a quivering mass of sputtering and moaning man on his bed.

Abe thrust up into his mouth, then grabbed his head. "Coming!"

Dom figured Abe thought he didn't like the taste since he'd pulled Abe off his own before—but he just hadn't been sure Abe was ready for a mouthful of spunk.

But he sure as hell was, so he sucked harder and got his reward when the warm fluid filled the back of his throat.

Abe, who'd been making all kinds of noises before, went silent as his body became one taut line of muscle. He shook and came, and a sense of relief hit Dom hard.

Abe loved what they had just done. All of his doubts in that respect were gone.

He came up and watched as the haze left Abe's face and he focused on Dom. A smile slowly stretched Abe's lips.

"Stay here tonight?" Dom whispered.

"Oh, yeah."

CHAPTER NINE

Abe stretched, legs sliding along the soft sheets. He rolled onto his side and pressed his face into the pillow. A smile tugged at his lips. He could smell Dom on the pillow, in the sheets. The man surrounded him, and it gave him such a deep sense of peace and rightness. He didn't want it to end.

Sliding his hand out, Abe came up with only cool sheets. His eyes popped open and he discovered he was alone in bed. The clock on the nightstand announced that it was after eight in the morning. He couldn't remember if Dom said he had to go in for an early shift. The bodyguard had admitted that he was naturally an early riser, which matched Abe perfectly.

But for a rare moment, he didn't want to get out of bed just yet. His body was luxuriously relaxed after last night. He kept in good shape, but sex with Dom meant using a few muscles that had been neglected over the years. Closing his eyes, he replayed each kiss. Dom's moans and cries of pleasure still rang in his ears. He'd never known it could be like that.

Patricia and he had burned up the sheets when they were young, but it had been about pure pleasure when they were together. With

Dom, he felt connected on a deeper level. There was something in his stare, in the way he let go, the way he trusted Abe so completely, that made it so much more.

Stifling a groan at himself, Abe took a deep breath...and caught the faint whiff of bacon. Had Dom gotten up to cook breakfast? Abe pushed into a sitting position and grinned at the sight of a pair of loose basketball shorts at the foot of the bed. After a brief stop in the bathroom, Abe headed to the kitchen, where Dom was standing in front of the stove in the similar shorts from last night and an old T-shirt with the sleeves ripped off, showing off his amazing arms. To hell with breakfast—Dom was a mouthwatering sight. He'd thought the previous night's sex had sated him within an inch of his life, but his cock started to perk up as he stared. Apparently it was determined to make up for lost time, and Abe no longer wanted to argue with it.

"I really didn't think it was possible for you to look sexier, but you've accomplished it," Abe said, his voice still a little rough from sleep.

Dom looked over his shoulder at Abe and the strangely pensive expression on his face disappeared, the smile that he flashed heart-stopping. Dom was normally a happy person, but this was a different kind of joy shining forth. And it was humbling to think that he was the cause.

"I have a feeling you're more tempted by the pound of bacon I've fried up rather than my sausage," Dom teased.

"I think I proved otherwise last night," Abe said with a wink. Flirting with Dom was just too easy, too addictive.

Dom turned his attention back to the stove for a moment and flipped over a piece of bacon before looking over his shoulder again at Abe. He grinned bigger than life itself and shook his head.

"What?"

"I just can't believe you're here."

Abe chuckled. "This isn't the first time I've been in your house, Dom."

Dom rolled his eyes and turned his attention back to the food.

"No, I mean I can't believe you're standing in my kitchen, half-naked, wearing a pair of my shorts after a night of incredible sex."

Abe could feel his cheeks warm slightly as he closed the rest of the distance between them. "Incredible, huh?" Dom had said as much last night, but it was still encouraging to hear it again. His confidence hadn't been at its highest when he decided to give it all a try. But then Dom kissed him, and he forgot all about being nervous and insecure. He just couldn't get enough of Dom. Probably never would.

"Fuck yes," Dom groaned. "My knees get weak just thinking about last night. I'm totally ready to do it all over again."

Abe stood behind Dom, smiling. His cock was fully at attention now and ready to go just from listening to Dom talk. Sliding his hands under Dom's T-shirt, he ran them up his wide, muscular back, loving the feel of his smooth skin. "Then why aren't we?"

Dom's head jerked around, holding Abe with his narrowed gaze for a moment, before he lurched forward again. He snapped off each of the burners with a quick twist. "We'll figure out breakfast later," he muttered under his breath.

Stepping backward so that Dom could move without hindrance, Abe laughed to see his desperate urgency. "Are you sure—"

He barely got the words out before Dom's mouth was on his, devouring him. It was as if it had been months since they were last together rather than just a few hours.

They hit the stairs and Abe pressed him into the wall, kissing back. Dom had obviously been sneaking bites of bacon. It tasted damn good on his tongue.

Laughing, Dom pulled away to tug him up the stairs behind him, but his ass looked so good in the shorts, Abe kept reaching out to squeeze those round cheeks and the third time, Dom nearly tripped. Cracking up, he turned, still a step above him, and wrapped both arms around Abe's neck to thrust his tongue back into Abe's mouth

"Abe?"

"Yeah." He bit at his bottom lip, then sucked it into his mouth.

"You wanna fuck me this morning?"

"Oh God," he groaned, reaching around to palm Dom's ass again and grind him against his abdomen. "Yeah, yeah I do."

"Then hold that thought." Dom kissed him one more time, lips lingering, before he hurried into the master bedroom and kept going. When he disappeared into the bathroom, Abe felt a return of nerves as they scrambled about in his belly. He went into the guest room bath and breathed a sigh of relief when he spotted the spare toothbrush and toothpaste in the top drawer. He cleaned up from the night before with a rag and soap. His hand was shaking with excitement, and he laughed at his reflection in the mirror.

Forty-nine years old and giddy as a teenager about to get laid.

He made it to the bed before Dom came out, still fighting the tidal wave of nerves rushing through him. He knew what Dom was doing in that bathroom.

Fuck.

Dom came out, gloriously nude, his dick already hard. He saw the direction of Abe's gaze and winked. "Just thinking about this kept it going." He grabbed a condom and lube out of the drawer, and Abe couldn't help but take in every curved muscle of his crazy-toned body. "Jesus, how much do you work out?"

"Have to be fit for what I do."

"You're sure as hell that. You make me want to up my workout."

"If you are in any way hinting that your body isn't perfect the way it is, I don't want to hear it." He pointed at the spike still aimed at Abe. "I have never met anyone who turns me on like you do. Ever. All you see here"—he waved a hand down his body—"is yours."

He crooked his finger. "Then bring my body here."

Dom climbed on top of him, straddling his waist. He picked up Abe's hand and squeezed lube onto his fingers. "I started the program in there already, so it won't take much, but you should explore first and yeah, probably get me a little more loose for that fat cock of yours. Damn, that thing's a beaut."

Abe was pretty sure it would be impossible to get any more

excited than he was in that moment. He slid his hand under Dom, brushing his palm on his hanging balls, watching as Dom's eyes closed and his mouth fell open. He didn't take his eyes off the man as he rubbed two fingers around his rim, then slowly slid one finger inside him. Hot. Holy shit, he was hot in there. And tight. He may have cleaned and loosened himself up in the bathroom, but that sure as hell didn't feel like it would work around Abe's dick.

"It'll fit."

His eyes flew open wide.

"Yeah, I can read your mind. Especially right now with that line splitting your forehead." He ran his finger down it. "I like-a the buttsex."

A laugh jumped from his throat and like that, he stopped worrying. The wicked twinkle in Dom's beautiful green eyes drew him in just as it had in the beginning. He'd been drawn to the man's sex appeal, yeah, but that humor was like fluffy icing on the best chocolate cake. A little extra flavor on the best taste. Laughter in sex wasn't something he'd ever experienced, and he found he liked it.

A lot.

"Put another finger in," Dom whispered.

Oh God, those words were so damn sexy, Abe's breaths picked up. He pulled out his finger, then slid in two and the tight clasp around them made him see stars. He simply couldn't wait to get his dick in there.

"Ready?" Dom groaned out the word. "I am. I so fucking am. Let me suit you up, gorgeous."

He scooted back and tore open the condom packet with his teeth, then rolled the rubber down Abe's cock, which reared in his hand.

"Damn. He's ready to go."

Whatever word that tried to come out of Abe's mouth then didn't work, and it only made Dom laugh softly as he held up Abe's dick. He rubbed the tip over his hole once, twice, and Abe made another sound—this one long and low—as Dom sank down onto him.

His head snapped back, the muscles in his neck going taut.

That. Felt. Amazing.

"Oh fuck, oh shit, Abe!" Dom came down to kiss him, his tongue sliding hard and fast into his mouth. He kissed him as he worked himself slowly onto Abe, and Abe was pretty sure he was about to come unglued.

Then Dom squeezed him in a hot, tight grip and he did.

"Agh!" he yelled and clutched onto Dom's hips. He couldn't stop himself from thrusting up into Dom, who yelled with him. Worried he'd hurt him, he forced himself to stop. "You okay? Did I hurt you?"

"No. Stings but that's a part of it. You can move—just go a little slow at first while I get used to you."

Abe groaned at the sexy words, his fingers digging into Dom's skin. He slowly rocked his hips, hoarse cries escaping his throat at how it felt inside Dom. It was like a vise, and he just knew it would be velvety without the condom, and he hoped for that at some point.

He was so *not* the kind for casual sex.

And this felt too incredible and anything but casual.

Dom reared back and used his knees to make himself rise and fall. Abe watched his dick disappearing into that hole, but couldn't see enough so he sat, wrapped his arms around Dom, and rolled them so Dom was on his back.

The man beneath him merely smiled and bit the corner of his lip.

Abe scooted up, holding his dick and at this angle, he could see Dom's hole swallowing around it as he pushed inside. He invaded that stunning body slowly and surely and nearly choked on his own tongue at how unbelievably hot it was to watch the man taking him. He glanced up to find Dom's gaze on him and they locked. All traces of humor were gone on his face as he watched intently, eyes slit, mouth falling a little open with each thrust of Abe's cock. Abe remembered something he'd read about hitting a certain spot better at a different angle, and he grabbed a pillow and shoved it under Dom's hips.

This time, when he pushed back in, Dom cried out, his legs falling open farther. "Yeah, fuck me, Abe."

Talk about coming unglued then. Abe's hips started snapping as he pushed in and out of that snug heat, unable to look away from the way Dom's body worked with him. Abs tightening and flexing as he rocked his hips up into Abe, arms flexed as he held his fists tight. And pleasure on Dom's face was something to behold, turning features that were almost pretty into a work of fucking masculine art. His lips were red, his white teeth biting on the bottom one, his nose flaring, eyes heavy-lidded.

Abe came over him, covering his body but propping himself up on his hands. His hips couldn't stop moving as he slid inside that slippery, tight hold. "It's good," he managed to get out between pants. "So good."

"Yeah," Dom breathed. "So full." He seemed no more capable of words than Abe. When he reached down and fisted his cock, Abe came back up, needing to watch. He grabbed the lube and squirted some at the base of Dom's cock, and the long, rumbling groan of appreciation made him dizzy. "Don't stop," Dom ordered.

He watched his face to see the right place to hit and knew he got it when Dom gasped and sped up the movements of his hand on his prick. Wet sounds added to how hot it was to watch that hand moving up and down, his thumb swiping over the top in a well-practiced move. Fuck, it was all just so...much. So raw and sweaty and...perfect.

"There. Right there." The veins in Dom's neck stood out as his head went back. Perspiration glistened on his smooth chest and along the scar on his left side. None of the scars on his body detracted from his looks in the least. In fact, the only thing they made Abe feel was angry that someone had hurt this wonderful man.

Dom's ass suddenly tightened around him and Abe grunted and fell forward, his own ass clenching in response as he watched Dom's balls draw up tight. "Fuck yeah," he breathed. "Let me see you come!"

Thick white ropes hit those gorgeous abs, and that was enough for Abe as his own orgasm erupted, the pleasure so intense, he gritted his teeth as every muscle in his body tightened, then released in waves of drugging pleasure as he came into the condom while still buried inside Dom.

When he could see again, he found Dom staring up at him, a fucked-out half smile on his face.

"Oh...did we find something we're good at," he drawled, his voice gritty and low.

Abe removed the condom, tied it off, and looked around. He spotted the small, silver trash can next to the nightstand just as Dom pointed at it. He collapsed on the bed and pulled Dom to his side, too. The air conditioner kicked on, and the cool air felt good on his sweaty body. They stared at each other for long moments; then a serious note entered Dom's eyes. He leaned forward and pressed his lips to Abe's in a long and affectionate kiss. When he pulled back, he sighed.

"I'm so glad you finally caved."

"Took me too long. And now that I know what I was missing, I feel like a fool."

"You're not. And I can't complain. I'm just so damn happy to have you in my bed. In my house. And in a moment, in my shower."

Abe rubbed at the wet hair on his chest. "I could use a shower."

Dom rolled off the bed and came around to Abe's side and held out his hand. "Come on. I'll show you how good I am at soaping your balls."

"My balls are going to need time, youngster."

"*Psht*," Dom breathed. "You haven't experienced my superior technique yet."

But Dom ended up being the one to learn a little something about soap and balls when he came all over Abe's legs.

Afterward, Abe took his time dressing, allowing Dom to head down first to the kitchen to see if he could salvage any of the food he'd been cooking. Belly grumbling, he'd happily eat anything that Dom could scrape together. But the ache in his chest bothered him more than the emptiness of his belly. The craving for Dom was getting worse the more time they spent together, rather than less. A part of his brain was shouting for him to hurry down the stairs and join him again in the kitchen. To sit down at the little kitchenette and just watch him at the stove, to soak in his joy.

Dom had made it clear that this wasn't some one night stand or meaningless fling. He seemed as invested in making a real go of... whatever this was as Abe was. But that was just it. Being with Dom like this, the overwhelming happiness and feeling of contentment, the rightness of it all...Abe could feel himself getting swept away and so quickly. It hadn't been what he was looking for. Not so fast.

Companionship. A little fun. Happiness. That had all been in the plan. But Dom was so much more. And he was coming to mean so much to him in so short a time. What if he got in over his head again like he did with Patricia? He'd gotten so lost in his ex-wife when they were young. With his experience, he thought he'd be able to better protect his heart, to put up more walls against getting swept up in everything that was Dom.

He didn't want to. Not really. His heart pounded when Dom was close, and he felt alive around him. The world didn't seem so daunting, and his life didn't feel so aimless. His joyful outlook and fierce determination put everything in perspective.

Maybe he needed to take a page out of Dom's book. Grab on to the happiness for as long as he had it and fight for what he wanted. And he wanted Dom.

Shaking his head at himself, Abe wandered over to the dresser and picked up his cell phone. At some point, either during the night or that morning, Dom had been nice enough to plug it in so that it wasn't totally dead that morning. A smile crossed his lips when his eyes fell on Dom's white Panama hat. The finely woven straw hat with the wide black band was striking on him, if a little odd. But the moment he flashed that rogue's grin and tipped the brim, Abe was a goner for the man. He picked up the hat to take a closer look at it and a piece of paper fell out, fluttering to the floor.

Abe quickly leaned over to pick it up but froze when he saw that the small sheet of paper was covered in the same stick figures he'd seen scratched into Dom's car and drawn across his garage.

The note was barely bigger than an index card but had significantly more characters drawn on it than the other messages. He hesitated for only a second before making his decision.

Snatching up the piece of paper, he placed it on the dresser and took a clear picture of it with his cell phone before covering it again with the Panama hat. He now had images of three full messages and the one partial message that Dom wiped off his front door. The thought of going behind Dom's back made him ill, but he knew the man was shielding him from the truth.

Dom's story of how he'd faked his own death replayed in his head. What had he gone through as a young man to make him take such a drastic step in order to escape? And was the person he escaped now leaving Dom the messages? Abe wasn't sure if Dom was just scared to tell him the truth or if there was a darker reason for him to hide it from Abe.

Sighing softly, Abe shoved his phone into his back pocket and hurried to the kitchen before Dom could come looking for him. He would help Dom whether the man wanted it or not.

CHAPTER TEN

The gun in his hand seemed heavier than usual as Dom stared at it. It was the same gun he carried when he was on jobs. He'd fucking carried it on countless assignments for Ward Security and after that first one working for Rowe, he'd never given the gun much thought. But this was different. Walking into this meeting, he wasn't a security agent for the preeminent Ward Security, protecting a high-value target. He wasn't even Dominic Walsh anymore.

He was John O'Brien. A petty thief and a con artist. John O'Brien wasn't worth a tenth of Dominic Walsh or even a hundredth of Abe Stephens.

That was why he'd escaped.

But carrying a gun into a meeting with his brother felt wrong. There was no doubt in his mind that the rest of James's crew would be present, and he had little trouble with the idea of shooting any of them to save his own neck. But could he shoot James?

No.

He couldn't shoot his brother. He might hate who James had

become, hate the kind of life that James was demanding he lead, but he couldn't shoot his own brother.

Cursing himself and his own weakness, Dom popped open the glove compartment and shoved the gun inside. He slammed it shut again. This meeting was not going to go well. He knew it in his bones. There was a nagging little voice in the back of his brain that demanded he call Rowe. His boss was the only one who knew about James and his past. Fuck, he should have called the cops and let them descend on the place.

But he couldn't because he was still clinging to the hope that he could find a way out of this. That he'd be able to return to the life he'd built at Ward Security and continue to date Abe. He was so damn close to having everything he'd ever wanted. It was like stretching out his fingers and feeling it all just brushing against the tips.

James wasn't going to snatch that away.

Climbing out of the car, Dom walked around to the front of the single-story, square building. The Joint was deep in what Dom was coming to think of as "old" Covington, across the Ohio River in Northern Kentucky. The city had pumped a lot of money into certain parts of the city to revitalize it for tourists and locals as a new place to shop and go out for an evening. But there were older parts where the money hadn't reached yet, where the streets weren't getting the quick pothole repairs and the blown lights weren't being replaced in a timely fashion. The shadowy places where the city officials turned a blind eye to its people. That was where The Joint sat. It was only natural that James felt comfortable in this part of town.

The smell of stale cigarettes and beer assailed his nose as Dom stepped inside the dimly lit building. He stood just over the threshold, blinking furiously to get his eyes to adjust to the darkness of the room. As it came into focus, he made out a small bar to his right with a limited assortment of bottles and a sprinkling of tables. Farther back, a set of lights shined down on the green felt of a pool table. A loud crack broke the silence, and the multicolored balls scattered.

James moved around the table, a pool stick in hand. He leaned over the table, lining up his shot. Another crack sounded as two balls hit, sending the solid orange three ball into the far corner pocket.

They'd loved playing pool as teenagers. It was one of the few times they'd appear in public together, though Dom was usually under a hat to hide his hair and partially shield his face from view. They'd joke and talk about their next score as they sent the balls flying across the table and into the various pockets. And then if they got truly bored, they'd hustle a few people, raking in several hundred dollars before leaving the hall. Those had been the good nights.

Now, James didn't look up at Dom as he continued to play, but that was just James's way of showing Dom that he wasn't concerned with his brother's presence. James loved playing with a person's head, and Dom had years of experience being both his target and his accomplice. It was just whatever suited James's mood.

Dom continued to glance around. It looked as if they were alone in the bar, but he knew that at least one or two of James's crew were lurking around somewhere close by. James might be insane, but he also knew how to take calculated risks. He always had a plan, an escape route ready in hand.

Taking a step toward the pool table, Dom abruptly stopped as he caught a hint of something else in the air. Possibly blood. His heart skipped a beat. Had they already killed someone here to take control of the bar? Very likely. But there wasn't much he could do about it until he was out of there.

With a frown, Dom walked over to the wall and selected a pool cue. He stood off to the side, watching as James lined up his next shot and pulled back the stick. James wore a plain black T-shirt that hugged his broad shoulders and thick biceps as they flexed with each movement. His face was blank, green eyes coldly locked on the table. A queasy feeling shifted in his stomach. He couldn't believe he was standing there with James again. There was a tiny chunk of his heart that was joyous to see him again. This was his brother. His own flesh and blood. They'd run the streets and hustled crowds up and down the coast of California for years. Together, they'd been unstoppable. Those early years had been free and fun because he always had James. And when he'd been young, he'd been sure that he'd always have James.

The balls on the table shot in different directions, and Dom followed the white cue ball around to where it came to rest at the far end of the table. Dom leaned down, lining up his shot. James's last shot had put in a striped ball in the side pocket, so he aimed at a solid. He hadn't played in years, but the stick felt surprisingly comfortable in his hands. With a semi-light tap, he sent the white ball smoothly across the table to just kiss the side of the dark-blue two ball, sending it into the top corner pocket.

"Dominic Walsh," James murmured. "Not a bad name."

Dom stepped back and rested the end of the cue on the floor while James circled the table, looking for his next shot. "It's worked for the past decade."

"Surprised you didn't dye your hair."

"Did for a few years in the beginning."

James stopped in the middle of taking his shot and smirked, though he still didn't look up at Dom. "People start to notice the carpet didn't match the drapes?"

Dom fought the urge to roll his eyes. There might have been a few blowjobs he enjoyed in those first years when people commented on the differing hair colors. He hadn't been ready to be remembered as a natural redhead. Someone of his stature was automatically recalled when he had flaming red hair to match, and he was trying to stay hidden. "Something like that."

After a few years, when he'd settled in the Cincinnati area, Dom let his natural hair color through, confident that James truly believed he was dead. What were the odds that James would ever come to Cincinnati? Apparently, they were pretty damn good.

James took his shot, but for the first time, the ball bounced around outside the pocket and didn't go in. The butt of the cue hit the ground with an angry thump and James straightened to glare at Dom from across the table. The overhead lights cast shadows across his face, carving in lines Dom hadn't seen before, aging his brother more than his thirty-two years. Life had been hard for his brother, but Dom had to believe that he'd chosen for it to be that way.

"You look good for a dead man."

A chill swept through Dom at his brother's words. They held cold rage and betrayal. And he had betrayed his brother. Abandoned him. Turned his back and left him to the life he'd chosen. The thing that Dom kept telling himself was that it was the life that James had chosen. Dom had wanted something else entirely.

"I didn't want that life."

"*That life?* You mean *our* life? The life that we had built. The one that we were meant for. That life? The one that you were suddenly too good for."

"You were taking it too far."

"Bullshit!"

"You killed that man, James! You killed him for no good reason and you know it! You went too far," Dom roared back at his brother.

It was as if they'd picked up exactly where they left off more than ten years ago. One of the last jobs they had pulled together had been a heist at a small jewelry boutique. It didn't have a huge collection of gems, but enough to make it worth their while. James had started carrying a gun—something he'd never done in the past. James had promised Dom that it wasn't loaded. He'd just flash it if he was trapped, and it would scare away any potential heroes. James had been running out of the store with the goods and a customer was walking in. The poor fucker was just in the wrong place at the wrong time. James fired two shots into his chest and ran over the guy. Dom later saw the report on the news. The customer had been half the size of James. His brother could have simply plowed through the guy and gotten away, but instead he shot him.

"It was about showing them that they need to fear us! It was about sending a message!" James lifted up the pool cue and pointed it toward the entrance of the bar. "Those people out there...they're just sheep. They're content to just stumble along through life and let the wolves of the world feast on them. We were not made to be sheep!" James lowered the stick and grinned slowly at Dom. "We're wolves."

Around him, one voice after another lifted up in a chilling howl from the deeper shadows of the bar. They came from all around him, proving that James's crew had circled them while they played pool. He took a sliding step backward, jerking his head around to try to spot the others in the bar, but his night vision was shot after staring at his brother across the bright light of the pool table.

"You crossed the wrong pack, John."

The sound of a shoe scuffing the rough concrete floor of the bar was Dom's only warning. With fists balled, he swung around and smashed his fist into someone's face before his vision adjusted enough for him to actually see his attacker. The person stumbled backward and crashed into one of the tables spread around the bar.

Another ran at him, lowering his shoulder so that it hit Dom straight in the gut. He staggered back several steps. Pain blasted across his stomach and ribs. The air rushed from his lungs and Dom struggled to keep his feet. Lacing his fingers together, he brought his joined hands down once, twice on the back of his attacker's neck before finally getting him to release his hold around his waist. Dom immediately grabbed a fistful of greasy hair and held his head steady while bringing his knee up. The man cried out and Dom tossed him aside in the direction of his first attacker.

Pivoting on the balls of his feet, Dom took a ready stance as the same man he met at the nightclub started to approach with his own fists raised. The handsome bastard's smile grew wider and his gaze focused over Dom's shoulder. A chill slithered down Dom's back before he could even turn around.

"You got this, babe?" the man asked.

"Wolves, John," James coldly repeated before pain exploded in the back of Dom's head, sending him straight to his knees. He tried to push through the gathering darkness, but a second hit sent him careening straight into nothingness.

∽

Oh, fuck, his head. Dom groaned and tried to shift, tried to reach for his aching skull, but he couldn't move his arms. He blinked slowly. His eyelids fought him just to raise even the littlest bit. Blinding light shot through his eyeballs and straight to the source of the pain in the back of his head. Nausea roiled his stomach and for a moment, he was sure that he was going to lose everything. Clenching his teeth, he forced in slow, short breaths, fighting back the pain and the queasiness.

After nearly a minute, the worst of it had passed and Dom slowly tried to open his eyes again. And the first thing he saw was James straddling a chair opposite of him, a wicked grin pulling his lips wide.

"There you are," James practically purred. "They even managed to knock the shit out of you without messing up this handsome face." James reached out and grabbed the sides of Dom's face, turning it right and then left as if he was inspecting it. "Except for this bullshit," he snarled when he caught sight of the long scar streaking down the left side of Dom's face. "What the fuck were you thinking?"

"I was thinking that I really didn't want to get blown up," Dom mumbled in a rough voice.

"See! This is what you get for going into this bodyguard bullshit. You have to worry about getting blown up for some little shit that isn't worth a tenth of our life."

"First, it was *my* life. Not our life. You don't risk shit for anyone but yourself," Dom said. "And second, I was there to save the life of a friend. Do you remember what those are? Friends? People you help and sacrifice for because you care about them."

"Who gives a fuck about friends when you've got your own pack?

A family that will do anything for its leader?" James rocked back, cackling.

Dom took a second to look down at the chair he was tied to. He frowned to see that someone had chosen zip ties over regular rope. There wasn't a centimeter of give in the ties. The chair might have been wood, but it felt sturdy as fuck. Hell, it could have been made by Abe—it felt so damn solid. There was no wiggling his way out of it. He needed to be left alone so that he could work on his restraints. Shifting his legs, he nearly sighed in relief to find that they'd left them untied. He remained still. No point in giving them a reason to tie his legs.

Of course, that was all assuming James didn't just put a bullet in his brain and call it a day.

"What the fuck do you want with me, James?" Dom demanded.

"You lied to me!"

"Only because you gave me no choice!" Dom roared back. His head throbbed and his stomach lurched, but he ignored both. Anger put fire in his veins, dulling the pain. "I didn't want to kill people. I wanted out. I wanted a normal life. Normal job. Normal fucking relationship. How the hell were we gonna have that as crooks? Always on the run, always hiding."

"You betrayed your family!" James jumped from his chair and tossed it aside so that he could get right in Dom's face. "You left us."

"Yeah, I left you and Dad because you wouldn't listen. I wanted something better."

"Nothing better than family."

"This is a waste of time," Dom muttered.

He knew it in his heart—there was no reaching his brother. They were both too hardheaded when it came to their ability to see no further than the idea they were clinging to in their brains. Growing up, they'd always been in sync. But by the time they were teenagers, he and James were constantly at odds. A part of him had hurt when they lost that closeness. James was his fucking twin. His identical twin. They should have always been in sync, thinking the same thing, feeling the same thing.

James sighed heavily, and Dom looked up to see him shaking his head. He walked over and grabbed the back of the metal folding chair to drag it back where he had been sitting before. "Dad was right."

"What?" Dom snapped.

"Dad said you were a sheep, but I didn't want to believe him."

"Oh, fuck Dad."

James's hand shot out, crashing into Dom's cheek and sending his head to the side. "Dad said you were soft. That's why I always pulled the hard part of the job. That's why you skipped around town, showing off that pretty face of ours as cover. You couldn't be trusted to handle the dirty parts, to make the hard decisions." James paused, his features twisting in disgust for a moment. "To pull the trigger."

"People aren't disposable, James."

"I didn't want to believe him," his brother continued as if he hadn't spoken. "My brother couldn't be a sheep. He couldn't be weak. He was *my brother. My half.* I believed that you were a wolf. I thought you were just waiting for that perfect moment to prove it to Dad." James shook his head and plopped back down on the chair. "But you didn't. You turned out to be a sheep and you *ran*."

"I didn't want your life. If I stayed, I would have been miserable and then dead."

James grinned a bit wildly at Dom and his heart gave an ugly lurch in his chest. "Then tell me, John, have you been happy?"

"Yes," he said without hesitation. Even without meeting Abe and falling for the man, he'd had a happy life in Cincinnati. He loved his job and he loved the men and women he worked with each day. He'd been incredibly happy...and now he hated to think it was all about to slip away from him. He really should have fucking called Rowe.

James chuckled and slapped Dom on the other side of his face. "Don't worry, brother. I'm not done with you yet."

"I'm not helping you with whatever the hell you've got planned while you're in town."

Winking at him, James stood but didn't step away from his seat. "Oh, I think you're going to be happy to help me when the time comes. But first we gotta take care of that mess you made of our face." Dom opened his mouth to ask what he was planning, but James was shouting across the room. "Slaney! Get your sexy ass back in here and bring that mirror you found."

A few seconds later, heavy footsteps echoed across the room. Dom looked over his shoulder as best he could to see the man he'd beaten up in the nightclub bathroom with a large mirror in his hand.

"You sure about this, babe?" Slaney asked as he came to stand next to Dom.

"Yeah, this dumbass went and got himself hurt. But we can fix it up easily enough." Reaching into his back pocket, James pulled out something black and gave it a flick with his wrist. A long silver blade slid easily out of the matte black handle and caught the light hanging over the pool table. With his free left hand, James dug a lighter out of his front pocket. A spark from the flint caught the fuel and a teardrop of light burned in front of Dom. His heart was pounding so hard in his chest; he could barely swallow.

"You can't fix my fucking face, James!" he desperately said. He struggled against the bindings holding him in the chair, but there was no getting free. Digging his heels into the floor, he pushed backward, trying to shove the chair farther away from his brother, but Slaney moved just enough sideways that his body was blocking his path. There was no escape.

"Grab his head and hold him still," James said.

Large fingers threaded through Dom's hair, getting a good grip before tightening. Pain lanced through his scalp and brought tears to his eyes. Slaney pulled back and to the right, forcing Dom to turn his head to a particular angle or risk having a huge chunk of his hair ripped out.

James moved the flame back and forth over the edge of the blade, heating it while staring at Dom. "Sometimes we have to make sacrifices if we want to keep our edge," James said.

He looked over to the mirror that Slaney was holding up in his free hand. James's wild green eyes jerked back and forth between the mirror and Dom's scarred cheek. He took a couple of deep, ragged breaths before tossing the lighter to the ground. Lifting the blade to his own left cheek, he dug in deep, cutting from his temple, across his cheek, to his jaw. Flesh hissed and burned under the hot knife. Spittle ran from his brother's open mouth, but his hand never wavered in its course as he copied the long, ugly scar Dom had acquired in the service to his friend Sven.

Dom couldn't draw his eyes from his brother's madness. His heart ached, and his brain shied away from what he saw. How had it come to this? Why couldn't he just leave? Pretend he'd never seen Dom?

James lowered the blade to his side and smiled at his handiwork. There was only a little blood running down his face from where the knife had cooled too much to close the wound again. While the wound was angry and fresh, it was nearly the same shape as the one on Dom's cheek. In a short time and with a little makeup, the wounds would be completely identical.

Looking back and forth from Dom to the mirror, James frowned. "Keep holding him," James ordered as he wiped off the knife on the leg of his pants and brought it back to the flame.

Dom tried to jerk his head, hissing when Slaney's hand dug harder into his scalp. The man put the mirror on the floor and clamped down on Dom's chin, holding his head tilted up toward the light.

The low chuckles that left James's mouth as he bent over Dom made his skin crawl. Mad. His brother had gone completely mad.

Searing pain slashed through him when James dragged his knife along the healed scar on Dom's face. The smell of burning flesh clogged his nose and his stomach heaved. He tried to scream, but Slaney held him too tightly to even open his mouth. A low, throaty moan filled the bar.

"Be still," James snapped as he kept drawing the knife down Dom's cheek. "It needs to look fresh like mine!" He picked up the mirror once again, then nodded. "There. We're the same again. Back to the way it should be."

Slaney released Dom's head and he shut his eyes, the pain and fury so intense that he shook with it. "No," he gritted out, his cheek on fucking fire. "We're not the same. We may look the same, but we are not the same. I'm not you."

"No, you're not a wolf." James walked over to a table and stabbed the knife down into the surface so it stood straight up. He turned back to Dom and smiled, the new wound pulling awkwardly at his flesh. "But I can use you as a sheep. You'll help us get what we want, and then you'll help us safely leave this city."

"Go to hell!" He managed not to wince with the yell.

James grabbed the chair he sat in before and dropped into it again so that he and Dom were on the same level. He smiled a little, cocking his head to the side. "You could turn us in. Wouldn't take much. But in this lovely little life you've built, would you really risk the sexy salt-and-pepper Daddy you've landed yourself?"

Dom went perfectly still at the first mention of Abe. He clamped his teeth together and fought the desire to snarl and fling threats at James. He'd just watched the man scar his own face so that they were identical again. His brother wouldn't hesitate to go after Abe or anyone else in his life.

"What if I walked right up to him on the street? Would he know it wasn't you? How long do you think it would take for him to figure it out?" James lowered his head a little bit, grin growing wider. "A minute? Five? Or longer? Would he finally figure it out when I had him on his knees and I was sliding my dick into his mouth?"

"You fucking bastard!" Dom snarled. He lunged forward in the chair, but a hand came down on his shoulder, pushing the chair back down on all four legs from where it had rocked forward. The plastic ties sawed through his wrists, cutting through flesh, but he barely noticed. He could only see James's twisted face and hear his maniacal laughter as it filled the room. "You stay away from him. I will fucking kill you if you go near him!"

James straightened in his chair, a look of smug satisfaction filling his features. "Then it looks like you're going to do exactly what I say."

Stopping his struggles, Dom stared at his brother. Silence filled the room again. He would listen to James's plan. He would learn his role. And when the time came, he knew that he wouldn't hesitate to put two bullets in his brother's brain if it meant keeping this insane fuck away from Abe and the rest of his family.

CHAPTER ELEVEN

Abe's heart slammed against his ribs, his palms sweating like he was about to do something illegal. Might as well have been. His thoughts warred painfully in his skull because this was a betrayal of sorts. But his gut was telling him Dom was in trouble. He'd sent a text to the man, hoping for a funny response, and when Dom hadn't responded within a few hours, every internal alarm he had went off. Dom wasn't due to leave for a job until that night. They'd kissed for a crazy-long time in his entryway, and then Dom had promised to come by after sending some interesting porn, so they could act it out before he left for a few days. Abe had been looking forward to whatever deviant clip came from Dom's repertoire and it never arrived. He'd been looking forward to the part afterward more.

A year of texting with the man had proved he had little patience when it came to messing with Abe, and Abe didn't think a night of incredible sex changed that.

He wanted more of that sex. A lot more of it.

An unanswered phone call later, and his worry had skyrocketed. So here he was at Ward Security, about to ask his son's boyfriend for help with the pictures of the stick figures. He'd printed out all the images, and the papers crinkled in his fist.

"Are you gonna lurk in the doorway all afternoon, Dad?"

He jerked at the sound of Shane's voice and saw his son smiling at him just inside the IT room. "What are you doing here?"

Shane put a hand on his chest like he'd been shot. "Not happy to see me?"

"Of course I am." *Just not ready for the shit show I'm about to unleash with my son present.* "I didn't think you worked here."

"I came by to pick up some papers from Rowe."

Abe glanced into the computer-filled room and shot a grin at his son. "Don't see the man in here."

Shane just rolled his eyes and waved him in. "You here for business or pleasure or both like me?"

"Business." Abe had only been to the building a couple of times, once for an office party and the other to pick up Quinn. But that time, Quinn met him downstairs, so he'd never gotten a good look at the IT room. It was a surprisingly big area with a massive table in the center and three different workstations with multiple large monitors all attached to mechanical arms. There were two people in the room other than Quinn and Shane. Gidget was a small blonde woman who seemed to favor long skirts, because she wore one every time he'd seen her. Today's was so full, it covered the leg she had propped in her chair. Bare toes of one foot on the floor, spinning her chair side to side. Cole looked like he could be one of the bodyguards with his big, muscular form but like the time Abe had met him before, the quiet man merely smiled shyly.

Quinn waved and stood. "Hi, Abe."

Now that he was here, his churning gut told him it was a bad idea. All eyes in the room were on him as they waited expectantly for his reason for just showing up out of the blue.

He flashed back to that last kiss next to Dom's front door, when his lips had been sore and Dom had run the pad of one finger gently over his bottom lip. "I'll never get enough," he'd whispered as he leaned close and soothed Abe's lips with his tongue.

He shut his eyes, heavy emotion a hard knot lodged in his throat. Risking Dom's anger was nothing compared to how he'd feel if something bad happened to him.

A hand touched his arm. "Dad, is everything okay?"

Opening his eyes, Abe smiled, then squeezed his son's shoulder. It was time to come clean. He walked to Quinn and handed him the sheets of paper. "I wanted to see if you could help me figure out what these mean."

Quinn looked at each page, his brow creasing. He wore jeans and a white T-shirt with a wrinkled blue button-down left open over it. His eyes suddenly shot wide. "Hey, I've seen these before. Hollis brought in a message and I couldn't do anything with it—not without more to go on. How many do you have? Are there more?"

"Just the ones there. Three and a partial."

"Where did you get these?" Quinn frowned at him.

Abe shoved his hands into the pockets of his jeans. He looked at Shane, whose face was twisted with real concern. And confusion.

"Okay. Just hear me out, because this feels like a betrayal," he said, his voice rusty. He cleared his throat. "Coming here like this. But he's not answering his phone, and we were supposed to talk earlier. He was coming over. You should have seen his face when the first one showed up on his door. He was terrified, but he tried to hide it from me." Fuck, he was rambling.

Shane stepped close. "Who tried to hide it from you, Dad?"

He took a deep breath. "Dominic Walsh."

Out of the corner of his eye, he saw Quinn's mouth fall open, but his gaze was glued to his son's face as his confusion increased before understanding smoothed it out. And like Abe had expected, a frown followed.

"You're the guy Dom's been pining over for a year?" Quinn asked, chuckling. "Go, Dom," he murmured.

Gidget and Cole had both stopped working—the room eerily quiet.

Shane crossed his arms. His mouth opened, then snapped shut. He opened it again, the pause so long, it grew uncomfortable. Some kind of electronic device kicked on and yet still, that silence went on. "But he's my age," Shane finally got out.

Abe scrubbed his hands over his face. "You think I don't know that?"

"But...he's my age," Shane repeated. "I think he might even be younger than me."

"Same age, Shane," Abe growled in warning. He didn't want his son fixated on Dom's age. He was just getting past it himself, and there were bigger issues to worry about.

His arms dropped to his sides, then he shoved his hands into his jean pockets. He pulled them out and ran one through his hair.

"Look," Abe said, "This isn't how I wanted you to find out."

"Find out?" Dark eyebrows went halfway up his forehead. "It's serious? Like dating? Are you dating Dom Walsh, Dad?"

"Yes," was all he'd admit. If he was serious, if they both were, then Dom should hear that first. No matter how much he loved his son and didn't want to upset him. "It's not a hookup."

"A hookup? How is that even coming out of your mouth? *Hookup?*"

Abe narrowed his eyes, his temper perking a bit. "Look, I know this is weirding you out. I knew it would, which is why I hadn't said anything before."

"So you wouldn't have said anything if I hadn't been here? Quinn would have known?"

The sigh Abe let out was loud in the silence of the room. Silence broken only by the whir of hard drives and the muffled noises of a busy office outside the room. "I would have gone straight to you after asking for Quinn's help. I wouldn't do that to you, nor would I do that to Quinn. I'd never ask him to keep something this important from you."

"This important? So it is serious."

"What it *is*, is between Dominic and myself. When we figure it out, I'll let you know."

Shane's face darkened in a way Abe knew only too well. He braced himself, wondering if his son was about to piss him off.

Quinn shuffled his feet loudly, drawing both their gazes. "Shane, remember me telling you Dom had it bad for someone who wouldn't give him the time of day?" Quinn looked at Abe. "You said no a long time, eh?"

"Eighteen years is like this giant, yawning chasm of time—time he hasn't yet experienced. Of course I said no. But he's—" Heat crept up his neck. "Persuasive."

A snort came from Gidget, who quickly covered her mouth, amusement dancing in her eyes.

"Oh God," Shane moaned, covering his face. "I so did not want to know this."

"Look," Abe snapped. "I'm sorry you're finding out this way. I am. But I'm not some decrepit old man, and Dom is old enough to know what he wants."

"And he wants your dad, Shane. I knew whoever it was meant something to him. Even you know Dom and how he liked to get around. It would take someone pretty damn special to yank him to a complete stop." Quinn offered Abe a sweet smile. "I get why he's so smitten. You're a great guy."

"He's my father." Even Shane must have known that argument was lame when a rueful smile twisted his lips. "This is going to take me some time to compute. I was picturing someone more like—"

"More like me?" Abe's chuckle didn't hold a lot of humor. "Trust me, I'm as shocked by all this as you are. And like I said, I don't know what it is exactly we have going on. I just know I like it. I like *him*. And something is wrong. I have the strongest feeling that he's in danger."

Quinn jerked his face down to the papers as if he'd forgotten them. "Danger. Damn. Okay, so let me look at these and the one

Hollis brought. It has four of the same figures as these other messages. The one he brought had been left on the wall outside the jeweler."

"I'm familiar with the case. The store owner hired us when the cops brushed it off as a child's graffiti. Hollis figured between you three, we'd get an answer." Shane stared at Abe, his eyes a little shocky.

He was still talking, so that was a plus as far as Abe was concerned. Shane had a tendency in the past to go silent when he was angry. Abe knew this was going to be weird for his son for a while, and he had no idea what to do about it. But right then, his concern was Dom and the messages.

Cole stood and walked over to Quinn. "May I?" he asked, gaze on Abe.

"Sure. I'm already deceiving him just by being here. I'd appreciate any help I can get so we can figure it out quickly."

Shane's shoulders slumped. "Dad, did he ask you not to say anything about this?"

"No."

"Then you're not really betraying him."

"He doesn't know I have the pictures, though. The first one was in chalk on his door. He smeared it before I could sneak a picture of it. The second was painted on my garage door the next day."

"On yours?" This time, real alarm coated Shane's question.

Abe nodded. "Dom came back—must have been really early in the morning—to paint over it, but I took the pictures after he left my place upset. The third..."

Quinn growled. "The third was obviously carved into his beautiful car. Assholes."

"You think it's more than one person?" Abe asked.

"I have no idea and this picture isn't the clearest image."

"He was on the porch at the time and it was pretty late. I couldn't get a clear image without alerting him to what I was doing. I just had this gut feeling the figures were important. And then, the way he's acted each time—it was obvious he knew exactly what this was about."

"What about this fourth one?" Quinn asked.

"I found it in his...er, house. This morning."

"Oh God," Shane moaned, closing his eyes before snapping them open. "I'm an adult and logical, but this is still..." he trailed off and then snapped his shoulders straight. "Let's see what we can figure out." He was suddenly all business as he took one of the pages from Quinn.

Cole was still frowning at the first page when he cleared his throat. "This reminds me of a show I saw years ago. A Sherlock Holmes show. I can't remember what it was called, but there were figures like these and they were secret messages that came from a gang of criminals."

"Criminals?" Abe thought about the aborted story Dom had told him last night. He wasn't about to share any of that, but it would make sense. Someone faking their own death would probably be running from someone bad.

"They're ciphers." Quinn nodded. "Let's take this to the table. We can put it up on the whiteboard." He grabbed the pages from Cole and Shane and started copying the images on the massive whiteboard in a black marker. Under each image, he placed a little line as if they were playing a game of Hangman. Abe followed the rest of the team to the table as they quickly shoved aside an empty pizza box and a jumble of paper plates and napkins. Shane took a seat beside him and placed his hand on Abe's, squeezing gently.

"We'll figure this out. I promise."

Quinn stepped back, tapping the marker on his lips as he stared at what he drew. "There are a lot of repeating images here. Even the one where you got only a partial, it looks like the prick was using the same images, so I think it's safe to guess that the first four images of the message from Dom's door are the same as the others." Quinn quickly filled in the missing images and stepped back again.

"So, where do we begin?" Shane asked.

"Well, all words have vowels, so they are a good starting point," Gidget said.

"Hey Gidget, I've got that—oh! Sorry!"

Everyone looked up to see a flustered young man standing in the open doorway. Dark glasses framed light brown eyes. He was actually wearing a suit and tie, carrying several files in his hand. Abe couldn't recall ever seeing anyone at Ward Security wearing a suit, not even the CEO.

"Sorry, I didn't know you were busy," he mumbled, starting to backpedal out of the room.

"No, wait! Daniel, you're good with puzzles," Gidget quickly said, waving him into the room. She turned to Abe and gave a little smile. "Daniel works in our accounting department, but he's got some experience in financial forensics and fraud. Lots of decoding strange things."

"I'm good with numbers," Daniel said a bit stiffly as he walked over to the table. He looked up at the whiteboard they were all facing, and his mouth fell open a little. "*Oohhh*...you're cracking a code. Looks like it's just a simple substitution cipher rather than a *Vigenère*, so it shouldn't be too hard."

"A what?" Abe asked.

"How can you tell?" Cole added.

"By the letter frequencies. You can see by the distribution of characters on the board that some characters appear more often than others. With a *Vigenère* cipher, you actually have two or more ciphers for a single letter, resulting in less repetition."

"Here," Quinn said, already walking toward Daniel with the marker held out. "It's obvious you know more than we do on this. You start and we'll help."

Daniel took a step backward, clutching the files to his chest and shaking his head. "No, really. I'm not an expert. It's just something that I've played with...for fun. I just do numbers."

"Please," Abe said, pushing to his feet. "Dom's in trouble. Cracking this code could help us find him."

Blinking wide eyes behind his glasses, Daniel's mouth bobbed open for a second. "Dom's in trouble?" He looked back at the board, nodding once. Snatching up the marker and putting his files on Quinn's desk, he stepped up to the board.

"Should we start by listing the entire alphabet and then marking letters off?" Gidget suggested.

Daniel shook his head. "That would leave us wasting time on letters that have a low chance of showing up. The best place to start is always with etaoin shrdlu."

"That was not English," Quinn muttered, dropping into an open seat next to Shane with a pad of paper in front of him.

"No, it's actually the most commonly used letters in plain English," Daniel said, looking over his shoulder with a small smile. He wrote the twelve letters on the board to the side. "We start by matching the letter 'e' with the most commonly appearing symbol and then seeing if it looks like it makes sense. If not, we continue down the list."

Cole suddenly laughed. "You know, we could feed this into the computer."

"I can't believe you didn't do that first," Shane murmured, gazing at his boyfriend. "It's usually technology first with you, babe."

"Well in this case," Quinn responded, pushing up his glasses. "Our brains may be faster. Like Daniel said, this looks to be a simple cipher. Something kids would make up."

"Kids or not, we're starting from scratch," Gidget said as she continued to try out the main twelve letters against the symbols until words started to appear.

It didn't happen nearly as fast as Abe would have liked. He got up and paced a few times, and Cole left once to get them all coffee. Noises from the first floor after about an hour made Abe wonder if there was a cage fight going on. Quinn only smiled and said something about a bet between two of the bodyguards involving the superiority of *Jeet Kune Do* versus *Muay Thai*.

At two hours, Quinn suddenly made a noise as all the color bled from his face. He looked at Abe. "I know what these say."

Gidget was nodding and jumping out of her chair to leave the room.

"Where is she going?" Abe asked, the alarm that had been simmering all day roiling to a full boil.

"Probably to get Rowe," Cole murmured.

Abe looked up to see a very pale Daniel already filling in the last of the letters they'd been missing.

DEAD MAN WALKS
DEAD MAN DATES
DEAD MAN CHOOSES
DEAD MAN'S ~~LOVER~~ – THE JOINT NOON

He stepped back. "The one we thought was the fourth message, must have been an earlier one. I think after he dropped off the message, he keyed DEAD MAN CHOOSES into Dom's car."

Abe came up out of his seat. "Lover is struck through on the third one then," he whispered.

Shane stood and put his hand on Abe's arm, squeezing his elbow. "Dad, that's a threat against you."

The panic that shot through Abe curled his stomach. "He met the fucker who left these messages because they threatened to kill me." It wasn't a question. He was trying to swallow down the fact that Dom was possibly in danger, trying to protect him. "I wouldn't want him to do that."

"And he probably knew that," Quinn said, his voice low. "I'm sure that's why he didn't tell you what was going on."

"This is bad." Understatement, but he was having trouble accepting this.

"What's bad?" Rowe asked as he strode fast into the room. "Gidget said I was needed in here." He walked to the whiteboard and stared at the writing. His lips tightened more and more as he read. "Someone needs to fill me in and do it fast."

"It's Dom." Surprisingly, Shane spoke up. He went on to tell

Rowe everything, paying particular attention to the message that was on Abe's garage—DEAD MAN DATES—and the one they now believed was the last. DEAD MAN CHOOSES

That was the one that was tearing Abe's heart to shreds. "We have no idea who is writing these messages—" Abe started to say.

"I do." Rowe's hands curled into fists. "And yeah, this is bad. Really fucking bad. Dom took me into his confidence when I hired him, but if he's gone to meet who I think he has, we have to move now." He jogged toward the door, throwing over his shoulder, "Quinn, figure out where this Joint is. Use the GPS on Dom's phone if you have to."

"Wait!" Abe's bellow bounced off every wall in the room. "If he's in danger, I want to know. Especially because it looks like this is my fault."

Rowe, who had stopped at the yell, turned. He eyed Abe. "Does Dom mean something important to you?"

"Yes. Very." He didn't even hesitate. Didn't have to think about it. "Who did he go to meet?"

Rowe looked around the room, his frown so fierce, his eyes were mere slits. He seemed to make some kind of internal decision because he nodded. "Dom has an identical twin brother and he's a psychopath. A psychopath who thought Dom was dead." He pointed to the words on the wall.

All of it made sense then. He walks, he dates…he chooses. Meet the brother or Dom's lover dies.

"If Dom kept that noon meeting today," Rowe said, his tone heavy with worry, "we'll be lucky if he's still alive."

CHAPTER TWELVE

Abe climbed out of Rowe's SUV, ignoring the other man's warning glares. He felt lucky the security company owner hadn't duct taped him to a chair and left him back at the office. It certainly sounded like it was his preference. But after seeing Rowe's reaction to the news of Dom's brother being in town, there was no way in hell Abe was going to be left behind when it came to tracking down Dom.

Of course, they very nearly taped Shane down when Rowe wouldn't allow him to tag along. Rowe complained about too many civilians getting in his damn way. He simply promised that Abe would be safe with his people, and Shane stepped back. Clearly not happy, but Quinn explained that he'd be supporting the mission and Shane could follow along from the office.

Dom and Abe had parted ways shortly before noon, and it was already after six. That was six hours too many that he'd potentially been in the hands of his brother. Panic flowed through Abe's veins. He needed to see Dom, to put his hands on him and know that he was safe. And then he'd be happy to shake some sense into the man.

Why didn't Dom trust him with this information? How were they supposed to try to build something if Dom was holding back?

Swallowing a groan, Abe wanted to shake himself. This was not where his thoughts should be. He glanced around at the neighborhood and cringed. The broken-down buildings and boarded up windows didn't exactly scream safety and warmth. Trash clogged the gutters and the street was rutted and pock-marked with holes. Despite it being the middle of the day, no one was out and about. Around them rose up the sound of rushing cars and commerce, but in this little slice of the world, the people and buildings were forgotten.

"So, you and Dom, huh?" Rowe drawled.

Abe jerked around to find Rowe leaning against the hood of the SUV, his thick arms folded across his chest. His expression was anything but welcoming, which was a little surprising. Both Quinn and Shane had spoken of Rowe Ward on more than one occasion, and it was always as this teasing, practical joker with a mischievous streak a mile wide. He'd not expected to be faced with a menacing version of Rowe.

"Not that it's any of your business, but yes, Dom and me," Abe said sharply.

"Oh, it's definitely my business," Rowe growled. "Dominic is one of mine, and I look out for mine."

Abe stared at the man. It was as if all of his feathers were ruffled over the events surrounding Dom. He was seeing an older man *and* his brother was in town. There was no missing that Rowe liked to be in the know when it came to his people, his family. And the employees of Ward Security were definitely his family.

A smile tried to form, but Abe pressed his lips together, holding it back. In this rare instance, Rowe Ward was all bark and no bite. But he was willing to bet that would not be the case when they got inside the bar.

"This serious?" Rowe demanded.

"It's not a fling if that's what you mean."

Some of the tension eased from Rowe's shoulders as they relaxed just a little bit. "If this is just some little experiment for you, you need to tell him now. Don't lead him on. He deserves better than that."

"I'm not playing with him, Rowe," Abe snapped. He stared at the other man for a moment, who was watching him with one eyebrow raised in question. "I care for Dom. I viewed him as a friend before it became more, and I don't ever want to see him get hurt. But I won't make promises that I can't keep."

Rowe grunted. "Fair enough."

"If the love doctor is done with his session," Garrett teased over the earpieces they were all wearing. Rowe had grudgingly given one to Abe so that he'd stay in the know and be able to take directions from either Rowe, Garrett, or Seth regardless of where they were located on the premises. "I'm in position at the rear."

"Boss, there's nothing in the way of cameras to tap," Quinn said nervously. "It's like a black hole settled over a three-block area and the bar is in the dead center."

"Bird's eye is quiet," Seth chimed in. Rowe had directed him to settle on a nearby apartment building rooftop and check out the surrounding area through a sniper scope. It was both reassuring and unsettling to know that they had a sniper backing them up. Abe had never walked into a situation where he needed a fucking sniper.

"Well then, I guess my friend and I are just going to pop into this dive and grab a beer." Rowe pushed away from the side of the SUV and started to lead the way toward the bar just down the block. Abe fell into step next to him, trying to ignore the rapid pounding of his heart and the sudden dryness of his mouth. Dom did this all the time and managed it just fine. He could walk into this bar with Rowe, Seth, and Garett backing him up and come out safely again.

"Tell me again why we didn't just call the cops?" Abe muttered under his breath.

"And what would we tell them? That our friend has been missing for six hours and we think he went to a bar?" Rowe asked incredulously.

"Or that we think our friend is in the hands of a known thief and murderer?" Abe snapped back.

"And how would we explain that? We might be able to hand his brother over to the cops, but it would also mean handing over Dom, and that shit ain't happening. Whatever crimes he committed as a kid, Dom has paid for in his lifetime. I will not let him go to prison for that bullshit."

Abe sighed. "No, I don't want that either. I just want him safe."

Rowe surprised him by putting his hand on Abe's shoulder and squeezing. "I know, Abe. I know. We'll get our boy back."

They reached the front door and it wasn't too much of a surprise that it was locked. Rowe reached into his back pocket and pulled out a handy packet of lockpicking tools. "Picking the lock," Rowe said in a low voice to the rest of the people waiting on him.

"Is there any chance you could teach me how to do that?" Abe asked with interest as he watched Rowe fit the hook and the wrench into the deadbolt. When Rowe snorted, Abe couldn't help but smile. "Just out of curiosity, of course."

Rowe glanced over his shoulder at Abe and smirked. "Only if you promise not to tell anyone that you learned it from me."

"Boss, you're such a bad influence," Quinn chuckled over their connection.

"Got it," Rowe whispered triumphantly. He pulled the tools free and shoved them into his pocket again. He quickly got to his feet and looked over his shoulder at Abe, who had been using his wide frame to shield Rowe from the view of anyone looking in their direction.

With a nod to Abe, Rowe led the way into the dimly lit bar. Abe followed close on his heels, happy to let the more experienced Rowe lead in this situation. They barely got more than a couple of feet inside before a man jumped down from where he'd been sitting on a stool in front of the bar. He rushed over to them, one open hand raised.

"Hey! You can't come in here! I thought they locked that fucking door," he growled. He was a large, behemoth of a man with a massive chest and a slight gut. Abe couldn't tell the color of his hair in the relative darkness, but it appeared long as it was pulled back into a ponytail.

"Hey, man!" Rowe called back. "The sign out front says the place is open. My friend and I just want a beer." Rowe's tone was friendly, completely different from what he'd heard from the man since first meeting him back at the office. Even his entire posture had changed. His arms swung free at his sides and his gait was looser. The guy was a damn chameleon.

Abe glanced around the bar, his eyes immediately locking on a slumped figure in a chair. Red hair shined like a beacon in the light hanging above the one pool table. *Dom!* But he couldn't move. Couldn't rush to him to make sure that he was okay, that he was still fucking breathing. He wanted to scream.

"We're closed. Get the fuck out of here!" the large man shouted. He pointed back toward the entrance as he got up in Rowe's face.

"Dude, it's just one beer," Rowe cried, giving him a shove so that the guy rocked back on his heels.

"Fuck this," Abe snarled under his breath. As the guy was left slightly off balance, Abe balled his hand into a fist and delivered a powerful blow to the guard's jaw. The guy flew backward, falling onto one of the tables. The spindly legs collapsed under the man's massive girth, sending him sprawling to the floor with a groan.

Rowe cackled as he jumped on the guy and hammered him again, knocking him out cold. He then looked up at Abe from where he straddled the other man and gave a low whistle. "I thought Shane said you were an accountant."

"I am."

"That's a killer right hook. If that's how you take on the IRS, I'd be happy to hire you."

Before Abe could reply, there was another clatter of noise from the back. Something wooden broke and then there was a heavy thud against the wall.

"Garrett, report!" Rowe commanded, jumping to his feet. The

former Army Ranger looked ready to charge toward the back to save his guy. Abe was torn over following Rowe to back up Garrett and rushing to check on Dom, who had yet to move in the noise of the shuffle.

"Stomped this cockroach!" Garrett said with laughter in his voice. "We're clear."

"Go check on our boy," Rowe said with a nod of his head toward Dom. "I'll take care of our friend." Rowe reached into one of the pockets of his cargo pants and pulled out a roll of kitten-covered duct tape.

Abe didn't need to be told twice. Weaving through the various tables, he ran over to Dom's side. As he approached, he could see blood crusted in the back of his hair. Abe dropped to his knees in front of Dom and hesitated. Was this really Dom? Both Dom and Rowe had pointed out that James was an identical twin of Dom. Could Dom have captured his brother and then left to chase after the rest of the criminals?

But that didn't explain the other guy...

His eyes scraped over the man before him. Blood still oozed from wounds around his wrists from where he'd pulled against the plastic zip ties binding him. There were no visible wounds to his face, but his breathing was slow and ragged. Abe was afraid that he had injuries that he couldn't yet see. And then he saw the scar stretching down along the left side of Dom's face. The same scar he'd traced with his fingers after they'd gone to bed the night before. Though some fucker had cut a fresh line down its side.

This was Dom.

Gently, he laid his hand against Dom's other cheek, rubbing his thumb along his cheekbone. "Dom. Wake up. I need you to open your eyes, baby."

A low groan fell from Dom's parted lips. "My fucking head," he mumbled.

"Come on, Dom. It's Abe. I need you to open your eyes for me."

Dom's head snapped up and he immediately winced in pain.

"Abe," he gritted out. He scrunched his eyes closed for a second and then blinked them several times as if he was struggling to get them to focus on Abe. "Abe? How? What are you doing here?"

"I'm saving your ass." Reaching into his pocket, he pulled out a pocketknife to cut through the bindings. But before he could even touch the blade to the plastic, Rowe's hard grip wrapped around his wrist, stopping him.

"You sure that's our boy?" Rowe demanded.

Abe wanted to snap at Rowe, but he couldn't blame the man for his caution. Just a moment earlier, he'd had the exact same thought. "He's got the scar on his cheek. It has to be Dom."

"No! He cut himself! He fucking cut himself!" Dom started shouting. He violently struggled in the chair; Abe had to draw the knife away for fear of Dom rocking the chair forward and accidentally hurting himself on Abe's knife.

"Whoa! Whoa! What are you talking about?" Rowe placed both of his hands on Dom's shoulders, gently forcing him to sit still in his chair. More footsteps echoed across the room, and Abe looked up to find Garrett crossing to stand on the other side of Dom. A worried expression dug deep furrows in his forehead.

"Q, Seth, how we looking out there?" Garrett asked.

"Everything is quiet," Seth replied.

"Nothing on the police bands," Quinn added.

"Dom," Rowe said evenly, drawing Dom's desperate gaze back to his boss. Abe's heart went out to the man. He looked utterly panicked and terrified. "What happened?"

"James fucking cut his face. He's got a scar like mine. You can't trust the scar. We look the same again."

Abe's breath caught in his throat. He was still sure that the man sitting before him was Dom. Because he knew him on a deep level. And the old scar was still visible mostly under the new cut. Plus, only Dom would point out that James now looked like him, right? But if his brother was running around free, how long would it be before

James crossed his path, attempting to impersonate Dom? He was sure that he would be able to tell the two men apart.

"Fuck," Rowe muttered.

"Then tell us something that only we would know about you," Garrett said. "If that would make you feel better since you think we don't know you."

Dom's wide, frantic eyes darted between the three of them, pain clear on his face.

"How did we meet?" Abe prodded. He was sure that there was no way that James would be able to answer that question.

"I chased Rowe around the office in my underwear," Dom instantly replied.

"What? That's not how we met," Abe said.

Rowe just snorted. "Yeah, it was."

Dom looked at Abe and a little smile pulled at the corner of his mouth. "I was sidelined after getting injured helping Sven. I chased Rowe through the office with my pants around my ankles, demanding that he put me on a case, or I wouldn't put my pants on again. Rowe gave in and put me on Quinn's case, protecting him when things went bad. That brought us together."

Abe couldn't stop the smile that spread across his lips as he looked up at Dom. "It all comes back to you not wanting to wear pants. I really shouldn't be surprised."

"Oh, God!" Quinn moaned over the earpiece. Both Rowe and Garrett laughed while Abe could feel his face turning bright red.

Dom looked from Abe to Rowe and Garrett. "What? What am I missing? It's the truth."

Abe lifted the knife to the zip tie and carefully cut through it, watching to avoid nicking Dom. "Quinn is listening in. We're all wearing earwigs," Abe explained.

Dom cringed. "I guess it's time you have a little chat with your son."

"He knows. He was there when we decoded that stick figure cipher," he admitted as he cut through the last tie.

Reaching out, Dom cupped the side of Abe's face and pulled him in close. His warm lips brushed tentatively across Abe's as if he wasn't quite sure that Abe would welcome his touch. Abe immediately opened his mouth, capturing Dom's in a demanding, possessive kiss. He needed this, needed to know that Dom was truly safe and well. Dom melted, relinquishing himself over to Abe, letting his mouth be dominated.

Rowe cleared his throat, breaking off the kiss. "As lovely as this is, we need to get going."

"Are you calling the cops?" Abe asked. He winced as he pushed back to his feet. His knees definitely didn't appreciate the hard, stone floor.

"Boss, there was a body in the back," Garrett said, his voice growing hard and serious. "One shot to the back of the head, execution style. Probably the owner of the bar."

Rowe frowned at Dom, who was also standing with a protective hand to his ribs. He winced with each movement, and Abe was dying to get his hands on the man to make sure that he was truly okay. "I'll take Dom and Abe back to the office. Maybe see if Jude or Snow's free to take a look at him."

"I'm fine. I—"

"Shut it," Rowe snapped, pointing at Dom. "You're on my shit list right now. You get looked at and then fill us in on what the hell is happening."

"Right, Boss."

"Seth and Garrett will stay behind and wipe off potential prints. When they're clear, Quinn will put in an anonymous call to the cops."

"Agreed," Abe said, putting Dom's arm over his shoulder. He was sticking close to Dom. Regardless of what he'd learn in the next hour or two, he was not leaving this man's side. Though from the pained look Dom was giving him, Abe had a feeling it wasn't going to be easy to hear.

CHAPTER THIRTEEN

Dom felt like shit. And it wasn't just his aching ribs or his throbbing skull and cheek. He couldn't meet the eyes of his friends who were gathered around him in Rowe's office. It was by sheer luck that they managed to catch Rowe's friend Dr. Frost as he clocked out from his shift as a trauma surgeon at the University of Cincinnati Medical Center. Snow, as he was known to his close friends, managed to meet them at Ward Security and gave him a quick look-over. The doc estimated that Dom likely had some bruised ribs and a mild concussion, but nothing more. He pressed for Dom to go to the hospital for a thorough check, but he wasn't going to budge.

The hospital was dangerous. It put him out in the open and potentially away from Abe. And nothing was going to separate him from Abe, even if the man didn't want to see him again after learning everything.

Exhausted, Snow just threw up his hands, asking why he'd even bothered to show up if no one was going to listen to him. Noah swooped in and walked the doctor to his car. Dom could have sworn he heard the man whispering something about plans for a twisted baby shower later that fall to celebrate Lucas and Andrei's impending bundle of joy. It was enough to distract him, because the doc's low chuckle echoed down the hall.

Sighing softly, Dom risked a glance up at the people gathered in Rowe's office. Garrett and Seth were still on their way back from The Joint, but Quinn hovered near the door, while Rowe sat on the edge of his desk. Royce, who'd just gotten off duty, was leaning against the wall. And Abe sat on the big leather couch next to him, his big hand wrapped around his forearm, but above the bandages Snow had wrapped around his wrists. He'd shredded them in an attempt to get loose.

Closing his eyes, he just couldn't look at their worried expressions anymore. He didn't deserve it. Didn't deserve their concern. Didn't deserve to be there.

"Dominic," Rowe said firmly but gently. "What's going on?"

"I'm a fraud. I'm a fucking fraud," he choked out. He had to say the words. Had to purge all the lies like cutting off a rotting limb. Even if it meant losing the only family he had left. Even if it meant losing Abe.

"You're not a fraud," Abe said sharply.

Dom opened his eyes and looked over at Abe, but he was all blurry. Dom blinked and then looked away again, focusing on his own shaking hands in front of him. "I am. My name isn't even Dominic Walsh. It's John O'Brien. My brother, James, is my identical twin. Growing up in California, we looked exactly alike. We dressed alike. We even talked alike." He paused and snorted derisively. "I was even sure that we thought exactly alike."

Pausing, Dom looked up at Rowe. God, how he looked up to that man. Rowe had quickly become his hero when Dom came to work for Ward Security. Not only did he know everything about Dom's past and still choose to take him on as an employee, but he took the time to teach him everything he knew. Rowan Ward was fucking fearless. He protected his friends and his family with a ruthlessness that was both frightening and awe-inspiring. In the years since Dom had come to work for Ward, he only wanted to make him proud. But now, Dom simply felt like a failure.

"It's okay, Dom," Rowe murmured.

"My father was a grifter. He taught my brother and me what he considered the family trade. He showed us all his tricks, and then he convinced us to pretend to just be one person—James O'Brien. John didn't really exist. We were always James."

"But what about school?" Abe asked.

Dom shook his head. "We didn't go. Dad taught us the basics. We knew math for setting odds and taking bets if he was running books. We knew how to read and write for jobs, but that was about it. Rowe was the one who pushed me to get my GED." Dom closed his eyes. He couldn't look at his coworkers or Abe. The man he was falling for had at least one college degree and was hands down one of the smartest people he knew. Dom was barely fucking literate.

Abe lifted his hand from Dom's arm and brushed away a tear that had escaped from beneath his eyelid and was streaking down Dom's cheek. "I'm not going anywhere," he whispered. "I know what an amazing man you are. Your past isn't going to change that."

Dom leaned his head into Abe's hand, not wanting to lose that contact, but he was just getting started.

"In California, James and I ran cons for my dad. We were living on the streets. It was all we knew. Mostly, it was petty theft. We told ourselves that no one was really getting hurt. It was just a game." Dom stopped and took a deep breath. "It was often just the two of us, so we developed our cipher language of the stick men. We got the idea from a TV show. But that way, if we were on the run and separated, we could leave each other quick messages that no one else could understand."

"When did things go wrong?" Royce asked when the silence stretched.

"We were about seventeen or eighteen. James wasn't happy with the small scores anymore. He started getting more erratic. He wanted to carry a gun and go for bigger-ticket items. Especially jewels. They were easy to hide and transport. He also knew a couple of people who were pretty good fences. But jobs like that meant more danger. People were going to get hurt. Get killed. I wanted out. Told him as much." Dom dug the heels of his palms into his eyes and rubbed. "He wouldn't listen. Kept saying that we were one person. That there was no out. That we were going to run that fucking town and people would fear him."

"He's insane," Quinn murmured in horror.

Dom choked out a weak laugh and chanced a look over at the young man. "Definitely. I was scared. I didn't think he'd kill me, but there was no way he was going to let me escape. So, when he was out on a job, I set fire to the house we were hiding out in. Really torched the place." Dom chanced a weak smile up at Rowe. "I feel like you would have been proud of me."

Rowe nodded. "No doubt."

"I faked my death and immediately got the hell out of California. I bounced around the country for the first couple of years. Dyed my hair and changed my name. Took a lot of shit jobs, but they were all honest." He dared to meet Abe's eyes for the first time since he'd started talking. "I swear, since I left California, I've not stolen one cent from another person. I've begged on the streets when I was desperate. I've worked jobs under the table, but those jobs were legal —as busboys and janitors and whatever the fuck else I could find."

Abe ran his fingers over the side of Dom's face again, just beside the bandage covering the scar, as he met Dom's gaze. "You're a good man."

"No, I'm not. I didn't start out as one, and I hate to admit it, but I am damn good at lying. Damn good. But I have never once lied to you, Abe Stephens. Never." He broke off his gaze and swallowed hard past the lump in his throat threatening to choke off his words. "I started life as a con artist, and I feel like I never really left that shit behind because I never admitted to anyone where I came from. Rowe knew, but only because he dug up the truth. I didn't willingly tell him. I was ashamed of it all. Horrified. Ward Security is the only good thing I've done with my life. It's been my chance to make it up to the world for being such a horrible shit for so many years."

"Dammit, Dom!" Rowe swore, pushing away from his desk to stand over him. "You need to get it through your head that you've paid your penance in this lifetime." Reaching out, he tapped his scarred cheek with one knuckle. "Dying on a job ain't gonna help anyone or clear your slate. It's already clear."

"When shit went down with my family, did you turn your back on me because of my shitty past?" Royce demanded.

Dom's head immediately popped up. "Fuck no. But that was different—"

"Bullshit!" he snapped with disgust. "You've always got my back. You stepped up when I needed you. You always have. Your past doesn't change shit with me. Just tell me what you want me to do." Royce straightened from where he was leaning against the wall and extended his hand to Dom.

He couldn't help but blink at Royce's rough hand for a second before he grabbed it. Royce jerked him to his feet and pulled him into a tight hug, which surprised the hell out of him. Royce was not a physical, touchy-feely kind of guy in any way. He was a blunt, grunting asshole on the best of days. His support brought tears back to Dom's eyes as he hugged his friend back.

"I know I speak for Garrett and Sven and a bunch of the other guys. We've got your fucking back, Dom," Royce murmured in his ear. "You just say the word, and we'll help you take down this piss-ant brother of yours."

"Thank you," Dom choked out. He released Royce to find Quinn grinning up at him.

"Rowe's just got good taste in deviants," Quinn teased.

"Fuck, squirt," Royce groaned.

Quinn ignored him as he quickly hugged Dom and then backed off to where he'd been leaning against the door near Royce.

"All right. All right," Rowe said, clapping his hands together. "Now that we've had our Oprah, hug-it-out moment, we need to get down to business and figure out what the fuck this bastard is up to in our city."

Dom nodded and returned to where he'd been sitting on the sofa. He couldn't quite meet Abe's gaze. The man had been amazing through it all. So damn supportive. But that was just who he was. He didn't want to see anyone hurting. Always there to help. But what about later, when all of the information finally soaked into his brain and he'd had time to mull it over? Would he really want to date someone who cheated, lied, and stole from innocent people? Would he feel like he could truly trust Dom? They would have to talk in private, and Dom was not looking forward to that conversation either.

"James is still crazy," Dom started again. "Actually, I think he's become even more insane over the years. And he's got a crew. From what I can tell, there's at least six of them, plus James. I can give some descriptions, but no names except for someone named Slaney. I'd say that's his boyfriend. I saw them all at Jubilee about a week ago."

"I can pull up cameras in the area of Jubilee and see what I can find," Quinn quickly offered.

Dom shook his head. "It was the night of that big rainstorm. Not sure if you're going to get much that's usable. But you can just start by looking for a guy that looks a hell of a lot like me traveling with people you don't recognize."

Quinn slowly released a deep breath. "It's not great, but it's a start." Looking over at Rowe, he cringed a little. "Can I pull in Cole or Gidget for this? It's going to take some really special search coding to go quickly through all the data."

"Grab them both. The faster we catch James, the faster we make sure that Dom stays safe and out of the hands of the cops."

"You know that's the most logical answer to all of this," Dom said, weariness creeping into his voice.

"What? The cops?"

"Yeah, I go straight to the cops and tell them everything."

"No! Absolutely not."

"Rowe—"

"You pour your heart out to the cops, and they're going to ship you straight back to California, regardless of the statute of limitations on your past crimes. They're going to try like hell to tie you to other bullshit your brother pulled, and you're not getting tangled up in his shit."

"Plus, that leaves your brother behind and loose here," Royce added. "If you're gone, do you honestly think he'll leave Abe alone?"

Dom's heart stopped for a second in his chest as he looked at Abe. He knew that Rowe and the rest of Ward Security would guard Abe with their lives, but he couldn't stand the idea of being separated from Abe. He wanted to be there to keep him safe, even if it was his fault that he was in danger in the first place.

"What do you think?" Dom asked. His voice sounded like his throat had been rubbed raw with a cheese grater. "You say the word and I'll go straight to the police right now."

Abe frowned as he stared at Dom. "You know, it might be better to hear what options Rowe has at his fingertips." A slow half smile started to break through. "Quinn has told me on several occasions that he's pretty good at sneaky shit. Besides, Rowe promised to teach me how to pick a lock, and I really don't want to miss out on learning that."

Sucking in a deep breath, Dom could only nod. There were no words.

"Did your brother tell you why he's in town? Is it the jeweler that Hollis mentioned a few days ago?" Quinn asked.

"Yeah, Carrington," Dom said with a nod. "They got in this one-of-a-kind line of jeweled purses. Real exclusive maker and millions in gems. If they fence the purses themselves, they can easily remove the gems and sell them loose for a bundle."

"When does he plan to hit it?"

Dom shook his head and sighed. "Not sure. There was an argument that interrupted my brother punching the shit out of my ribs. He's got some techy guy on his crew that came in. Apparently, the store not only upgraded their security system, but the police have recently changed up their surveillance of the area. It sounded like they were planning to scout the place again before they knocked me out."

Rowe chuckled and muttered under his breath, "Freaking Hollis. The guy's still got great cop instincts. He must have told that Detective Martin to warn the jeweler that something was brewing."

"Will that be enough to get your brother to walk away?" Royce asked.

"Nope. He might back off for another day or two, come up with a new plan, but he won't walk away. Not once he's decided on a target. His reputation is at stake. Nothing can beat him. At least that's what he believes."

Rowe narrowed his gaze on Dom. "What does he want from you?"

"He wants me to be his double again."

"Join his gang?" Abe asked in horror.

"No, he doesn't trust me or even forgive me for betraying him."

Royce grumbled something less than flattering about his brother and his ideas of betrayal.

Dom swallowed down a snicker. He definitely hadn't expected this kind of support. "He wants me to take the blame for the heist...or he'll kill Abe."

"What the hell!" Quinn shouted. Royce was already stepping over, putting a comforting hand on the young man's shoulder, but Dom's attention was on the small tremor that went through the hand resting on his thigh.

"I'm sorry, Abe," Dom murmured. "I should have stayed away. Should have left you alone. If I had, you wouldn't be in this mess with me."

"Fuck that!" Abe snapped. "I wouldn't change a damn thing. He's not going to get anywhere near me."

"What about the safe house?" Royce offered. Royce's aunt had passed away and left him a ranch home on several acres of land out in the middle of nowhere. They'd used it a few times to protect their clients.

"I can't disappear," Dom said.

"Because your brother can frame you for anything he does unless we have solid proof that it wasn't you," Rowe added. He frowned at Dom for a minute, then gave a little nod as if deciding something. "You have to have someone with you at all times."

"I'll do it," Abe quickly offered and Rowe grinned. Dom looked over at Abe in surprise, but before he could comment, Rowe was already speaking.

"Sorry, Abe. But you're not my first choice. You're a target too."

"I'm not leaving him."

Quinn stepped forward. "We can add more bodyguards. Have them both stay with Shane and me."

"Shane's place is a one-bedroom and you've got roommates," Abe said.

Dom sighed. "That's a little too cramped and putting too many people in danger."

"My old place," Royce threw out. "The security is top notch, and no one is currently living there. Plus your brother wouldn't know about it. Keeps you hidden but close at hand."

Dom sat up a little straighter, and a small grin spread across his face. "You finally moved in with Marc?"

Royce just grunted, barely hiding an answering smile. The man might not shout it from the rooftops, but he was utterly lost over Marc. Dom was sure that the official move was well overdue. Didn't matter fast or slow. Those two were meant for each other.

Grumbling to himself, Rowe pushed away from his desk and paced behind it, rubbing one hand through his hair as he thought, leaving it standing on end. "Royce's place is a start. I want you two to go straight there and stay," he said, pointing at Dom and Abe. "I need to look at the schedule, but I'll be sending over guards. At least one will be in the house with you at all times."

He then turned his attention over to Quinn. "In the meantime, I want you, Gidget, and Cole combing the city to find James. Whatever it takes. I don't wanna know details. Just get it done. We need to lay our hands on the bastard and his crew before they can frame Dom."

"Got it, Boss," Quinn said before scrambling out of the office and down the hall, likely in search of his two coworkers.

"I'll go get the key for the place out of my locker," Royce said, following behind Quinn.

Putting a hand against his bruised ribs, Dom slowly pushed back to his feet. His body ached, but the dull pain was easily overlooked by the heavy thud of his heart. He'd never expected this from his coworkers, his friends, but he was beginning to realize that maybe he should have. In the time that he'd spent with them, he knew that he would do anything for them. Risk his life to protect and help them. He should have known that they'd feel the same way.

"Rowe—" he started, but Rowe cut him off by holding up his hand.

"If your next words are 'sorry,' I don't wanna hear them. I knew this day would come when I offered to hire you, and I didn't hesitate. You belong at Ward Security. No question about it. We'll catch this douchecanoe, and then you can tell me what the hell was going through your head to make you think you couldn't tell me the second you learned he was in town."

"Got it," he agreed, though he wasn't sure what he was going to tell Rowe. Well, there wasn't much to tell other than he was thinking that he'd protect Abe, but it still came down to the fact that he should have told Rowe from the start.

A strong hand landed against his lower back and Dom shivered. Abe. *What the hell was Abe going to say when they were finally alone?*

CHAPTER FOURTEEN

City lights and bright green trees passed in a blur as Garrett drove them to Royce's old house in a company SUV. Dom shut his eyes and rested his head on the seat—which caused him to wince. Feeling around the tender spot on the back of his head, he was glad he didn't have a worse concussion but pissed at his brother all over again. Exhaustion crashed through him, making him feel like it should be far later than the current eight in the evening.

He ran his fingers down the bandage on his cheek, the horror over watching James deliberately disfiguring himself coming back. Today, he'd looked into the face of pure madness, and it had chilled him to the soul. The young man who had looked at all they'd been forced to do by their father as a game was gone.

What the hell had happened to James after he left California? He'd been pushing boundaries they'd always operated under before, but this...this just felt so much more extreme. More frantic and desperate. Dom wouldn't have called his brother crazy when they were children. Would James have turned out this way whether he'd left or not? Would he have been able to save his brother if he'd stayed?

Dom's mind immediately skittered away from the thought the second it formed. There was no going back. No promises that he would've been able to change the course of James's life if he'd have stayed. Leaving had been his only option for survival, and James had forced him to take it.

Garrett, who'd arrived at Ward Security as they were leaving, kept shooting worried glances at Dom in the rearview mirror, but didn't say anything.

"You okay?" Abe asked.

Dom realized Abe was watching him from where he sat next to him. He sat up and despite the sting in his cheek, gave Abe his sauciest grin. "If you're worried I'm not up for some fun, don't be."

"I wasn't worried about that, Dom. I'm concerned about you."

"I'm okay. Promise. I really am up for some fun."

"Ew." Garrett said it so matter-of-factly, both Dom and Abe laughed. He pulled into Royce's driveway, which looked like every other driveway in the new neighborhood. "I'm going to wish I brought earplugs, aren't I? Just let me check the house before you two come in."

"I know the drill, G," Dom muttered. "And I'm pretty sure I can watch out for Abe just fine. I've got a few bruises and a cut—I'm fine. Had a doctor look me over before you got there."

"I'm well aware. Rowe filled me in. So let me do this without any griping from the peanut gallery. You can owe me." Garrett took the keys and got out of the car. He soon disappeared inside the house.

Royce had lived in a nondescript, unbelievably boring townhouse in Fort Thomas, Kentucky. Dom had been there, but each time, he was always surprised by the genuine lack of personality when its owner had more than his fair share. The exterior of the two-story was a nice middle-class place with a neatly manicured lawn and little ornamental shrubs. Like Royce gave a damn about shrubbery. Dom glanced up at the house and a little smirk formed. But then, if you were related to a notorious mob family and wanted to just blend in and disappear, this quiet neighborhood with its perfect lawns and cookie-cutter houses was a great start. Maybe he should have taken more lessons from Royce on hiding. James might never have found him.

"He a good friend of yours?" Abe asked.

He stared at the closed door, then watched the windows, knowing that when a light came on, all was clear. He'd watched Garrett move through an empty place before—the man glided through silently, like a cat. "Yeah, he's probably my best friend out of everyone at work. We're all close, but Garrett and I hang out the most."

"Ever played each other's wingmen?"

"Of course." Dom draped his arm over the seat, then laid his temple on Abe's shoulder. The energy he'd managed to scrape together just minutes ago was already draining out of him. "This was a shitty, shitty day, Abraham."

Abe turned and pressed his lips to the top of Dom's head. God, the man was just so affectionate. Dom was ready for a lot more of that attention. He didn't feel like talking anymore, hashing out anything else. He wanted a shower, food, and sleep.

"I wish you'd told me about your brother," Abe whispered. "About your childhood."

He didn't lift his head, but he closed his eyes. There was no missing the hurt in those soft words. "I just finally got you. Laying all that on your lap wouldn't have been fair."

Abe kissed his head again. "There is nothing unfair when it comes to you and me. Honesty is what I want from you. I want to know who you are, the good and the bad. And fuck, Dom, look what he did to you."

Dom's eyes popped open to stare at the strong hand that had come to rest on his thigh. "Well, at least I know the scars weren't a deterrent before."

"They never were and never will be. I just hate that he hurt you."

Abe's hands balled into fists so tight, the knuckles popped. "I want to get him alone in a room. Make him regret he ever laid a hand on you."

"I don't want you anywhere near him." Dom shut his eyes and tamped down a shudder. Just the thought of Abe being alone with his brother made his stomach churn. It wasn't that he thought Abe couldn't handle himself. It was that his brother was absolutely certifiable. There was no telling what James was capable of now.

"You said he'll try to come after me." There was a slow, pensive note to Abe's tone that nearly made Dom smile. His man was not one to make rash decisions, and Dom was finding that he liked his slow and steady ways. They were certainly proving smarter than his "jump in with both feet and figure it out later" style. "And I've been thinking about that. I may have an idea."

"Oh, yeah?" Dom lifted his head and opened his eyes. "What's that?"

"Let it percolate a bit, then I'll share. Let's just go inside and have that chili we planned."

"I want to shower first. Will you do it with me?"

Abe stared at him a few moments, the corner of his mouth going up. "Of course. I'll be happy to wash the rest of the blood out of your hair. It makes me sick to see it there." He ran a finger next to the fresh wound by his old scar. "I'm with Garrett. This infuriates me," Abe said, mentioning the first words out of Garrett's mouth when he met them at Ward Security. "Your brother is sick."

"It's why I ran." Dom turned his head away from Abe and stared out the window at the neat row of townhomes. "I shouldn't have left him out there to terrorize other people."

Abe carefully grabbed Dom's chin, forcing him to turn his head back to face him. There was no escaping those large brown eyes staring him down. "What were you going to do? Take out your own family?"

"I could have set it up so he was arrested."

Abe frowned and gave a little shake of his head. "You did what you felt was right at the time. You were young and he is still your brother. Self-recrimination is a waste of time."

Turning his head, Dom brushed a light kiss across Abe's fingers. "When did you get so smart, Mr. Stephens?"

"Probably about the time I gave in to your constant seduction."

A bark of laughter jumped from Dom's lips. "Seduction? Really? Felt more like begging to me."

"This old man was always flattered, Dom."

Dom looked around. "What old man?" He smiled again but knew it didn't hold a lot of humor. He felt icky and just wanted to be clean and feel Abe's strong body against his.

Garrett stepped outside the house and came to help with the overnight bags and groceries. Rowe insisted they all have satchels ready with changes of clothes and toiletries in the office because they never knew when they'd end up on a job. Rowe had grabbed one for Abe from one of the bigger employees. They'd stopped for chili and sandwich makings on the way, so they were prepared for at least a few meals while they discussed what their next step would be.

Royce said the house still had dishes and furniture—he wasn't attached to anything in it, which was sad. Dom loved his historical house because it came with deep roots—something he'd never had in his entire life. Of course, Royce was now moved into his boyfriend's house, which was warm and full of eclectic art. Definitely what Royce needed. His friend talked about listing the townhouse as a vacation rental rather than selling it right away. That was assuming they didn't manage to destroy it while using it as a safe house. Bullet holes and fire damage were great selling points.

They took the bags inside, and Garrett offered to put away the groceries so Dom could shower. He felt no shame in luring Abe to come with him. And when they finally stood in the beige-tiled stall, Dom realized that Abe's big body was good for more than hot sex. He was strong and solid, and it felt so damn wonderful to rest against him. Dom wrapped his arms around Abe and laid his unhurt cheek on his shoulder. Hot water pounded against his right side, where their bodies were plastered together.

"That's it," Abe said as he held him tight, bracing strong legs on the slick tile. "Lean on me. I can hold you up."

Dom would normally have too much pride to show this kind of weakness but for some reason, it didn't feel that way with Abe. It felt like he could be himself, could lean and be leaned on—that they could hold each other up and stand strong together no matter what came.

When Abe turned him and started gently shampooing his hair, feelings raced through him so hard, they swelled in his chest and he couldn't hold them in any longer. "I'm in love with you." His voice was low and soft, and for a moment Dom wasn't sure if Abe heard him over the pounding water.

The fingers in his hair paused, then lightly tugged his head back and to the side. Abe stared at him, a small smile pulling up one corner of his mouth.

"What?" Dom asked, shampoo dripping down his forehead. "Like it's a surprise?"

"I thought we were just going to try the dating thing?" Abe asked, something cautious in his expression—although the smile remained.

His heart started beating hard, and he worked to keep disappointment off his face. "We are. There's just an extra layer of feelings involved."

"Love isn't just an extra layer of feelings. Love is *the* feeling."

He searched those brown eyes, and what he saw in response chased away the disappointment instantly. That swell in his chest turned warm and welcoming, and he was glad for the water on his face, because his eyes teared up. "*The* feeling, huh? Like the big kahuna?"

Abe smirked. "That and the whole shebang."

"The grand poobah?"

"And the top banana."

Dom grinned and blinked as water got in his eye as he turned toward Abe.

"Love encompasses all those layers, Dom. Friendship, affection, desire...fear." Abe swiped his thumb over the shampoo right before it followed the water into Dom's eye. He touched the waterproof bandage the doctor had placed over his cheek. "Today, when I knew you were in danger, the fear that swept through me was overwhelming. Fear of losing you."

"So you're close to the whole shebang?"

"Close?" Abe chuckled and smoothed his fingers through Dom's soapy hair, pulling it back from his face. "I'm right there with you, Dom. But that fear is about more than just losing you. It's about loving you, giving you my heart when—"

"When what?" Dom broke in. "I get bored and move along? That's not going to happen. I'm in this for good. Hell, Abe, I knew I was in love with you before we even kissed. And I'm not trying to pressure you into saying something you don't fee—"

This time Abe broke him off. With movement. He backed him into the spray and tilted his head back into it, careful to keep the water off the bandage. He stroked his fingers through Dom's hair until all the shampoo was gone, then he smiled and shook his head. "Silly man. I'm already in love with you and probably have been since before we kissed."

The joy that shot through him threatened to send him to his knees. He gave Abe a half-watery grin, grabbed his head, and kissed him. Again. And again. He whispered against his lips. "We're so doing this."

"Yeah, I suppose we are," Abe whispered back. "Come on, let's dry off and get some food in you."

They stepped out of the large shower. Dom hurriedly dried off and slung the towel around his waist. He looked in the mirror, frowned at the bandage, then grabbed his toothbrush out of his travel kit. As he brushed, Abe walked behind him and it felt so domestic, warmth filled his chest. This was what he had to look forward to. Abe paused and watched Dom in the mirror and Dom watched him right back because damn, the man was fine naked. The wide shoulders and chest with its curly brown and gray hair, the muscular arms and thighs. And when Abe turned to drape his wet towel on the rack, his round, meaty bubble butt made Dom's hands itch to grab. He knew Abe worried about his body because of his age, but Dom loved it exactly as it was.

Love. The big guy loved him.

Abe came up behind Dom and brushed his fingers in the hair on either side of the sore spot on Dom's skull. "Have I ever told you I love your hair?" He wrapped his arms around Dom gently and plopped his chin on his shoulder. "How're your ribs?"

Dom quickly bent over the sink and rinsed out his mouth. "If you're again asking if I'm up for some kind of sex, yes."

Abe snorted, then nuzzled into Dom's neck when he straightened again.

Dom wondered if the man realized how gorgeous he was, how affectionate. That warmth spread through Dom's chest, and he set down the toothbrush and hugged his arms against Abe's, ignoring the twinge in his ribs. Lips kissed his neck and he tilted his head and closed his eyes. Abe took the lobe of his ear into his mouth and sucked on it before letting go and stepping back. "Turn around."

"Hold on," Dom murmured before bending to get another handful of water in his mouth to swish out the last of the toothpaste. His ass bumped into Abe's groin, and he saw the naughty smile flit across Abe's mouth before he grabbed Dom's hips and rubbed his dick against Dom's towel-covered ass.

Even with the slight throb in his head, his interest perked up. He turned around and gasped when Abe picked him up and plopped him—still gently—onto the counter. He then pulled the towel free to let it drape to the sides. Dom spread his legs and tugged Abe between them for a kiss.

"You scared the shit out of me today," Abe whispered against his mouth. "You're not allowed to do damn fool things like go off alone again."

Ooh, bossy Abe was fun. "I'm in danger like that all the time."

"Not like that, you aren't. From everything you've told me, your brother is a nightmare. You've got people who back you up on the job. You should have asked one of them or me to come with you."

"Did I tell you that seeing your face, seeing that you came for me, did something funny to my heart?" He ran the pad of his thumb over Abe's bottom lip.

"Did it? Maybe that's because it's mine."

Dom's belly quivered when Abe sucked his thumb into his mouth. He ran his tongue over it, then hollowed his cheeks and sucked on it.

"Fuck," Dom whispered, the word cutting off when Abe reached around him and groped for something on the counter. He came back with the lotion and he pumped a huge glob into his hand. "Okay," Dom breathed. "This is getting interesting."

Abe stepped close, making Dom widen his legs more, and took them both in his hand. He coated their cocks with lotion, his fingers tight as he slid his fist up and down.

Dom's eyes fell shut, and his head went back.

"Put your arms around my neck," Abe ordered in a low, gritty tone.

Complying, Dom scooted until his ass was nearly hanging off the towel-covered counter. He thrust up into that warm, slippery fist, his eyes rolling back in his head. "S'good."

"Everything with you is good." Abe twisted his hand every time he got to the top, rubbing their tips together. He kissed Dom's neck and opened his mouth over Dom's collarbone, licking the sweat that was starting to pool there and making Dom squirm harder. He came up and kissed the scruff on his jaw he'd been about to shave. "You are so fucking stunning."

Abe made him feel that way. He wondered if the man had any idea of how he looked at Dom. How he had been looking long before he'd decided to give them a try. When Abe suddenly tightened his fist and sped up his movements, Dom had to grab on to his shoulders.

"Yeah," he yelled before snapping his mouth shut because the vague thought of Garrett downstairs was slightly alarming. Not that he cared really—Garrett would know full well what they were doing up here in the master bathroom.

Abe was panting against his neck and coming up on his toes, his hips snapping in time with his hand. Dom was dizzy with how fucking hot this was—basically, getting jacked off on a bathroom counter. He loved that Abe was taller, so this even worked.

He grabbed Abe's head and brought him in for a kiss and when Abe did that thing with his tongue on Dom's bottom lip, he felt the tell-tale tingling at the base of his spine. He opened his mouth and moaned as that talented tongue entered his mouth. Abe deepened the kiss, still jacking them together, still with the sexy-as-fuck twist every time he got to the top. Dom imagined that was how he masturbated, and just that image in his head was enough to send him over.

Every muscle in his body snapped taut, and his breath shuddered once, twice, and then blinding pleasure hit him as he shot up between them.

"Hell yeah," Abe breathed. "Come for me, baby."

He gritted his teeth, managing to hold on long enough to watch as Abe's eyes flared open wide and a hoarse cry spilled from his lips. His big body bucked against Dom's as he came and kept coming.

When it seemed Abe's legs shook, Dom chuckled and grabbed on to him, wrapping both legs around Abe's back. Their mixed semen slid between them and it felt so erotic, Dom smashed his mouth onto Abe, who kissed him back with just as much fire. It lasted a long, long time—until Dom had to tear himself away to suck air into his lungs. He heaved and grinned at Abe, whose smile back was crooked and so damn beautiful, Dom caught his breath.

That damn L word was on the tip of his tongue, shaking and ready to jump so damn badly. He did. He loved the older man and in that moment, he knew he would do anything to convince him of it.

CHAPTER FIFTEEN

Abe left Dom crashed out on the king-sized bed in the master bedroom and went downstairs to start the chili. His stomach growled loudly as he walked through the plain living room with its white couch and wood coffee table. The kitchen held honey-colored cabinets with a gray countertop.

"There is not one thing in this place to give it any character," Garrett said as he chopped onions. He looked up. "Dom okay?"

Nodding, Abe washed his hands and worked to unwrap the pounds of ground beef and put them in a stew pot.

"So, Dom tells me you make hand-carved furniture and...how did he put it?" He paused with the knife in the air. "The coolest whimsical wood thingies that go in windows. I have no idea what that could be."

Abe snorted. "They're frames. You'd have to see them to get them."

"He says you're really talented."

"Nah, I just like wood."

When Garrett snorted this time, Abe felt his face heat. He stuck it over the now sizzling meat. "I should have known with you being Dom's friend that you'd take it that way."

"I'm a guy. I'm bound to take it that way. But yeah, when I can hear my friend shouting in pleasure from another floor in the house, my mind is going to naturally flow that way. So yes, I can with great confidence say that you like wood." He scraped onions into the pot. "I've met your son. He get his smartass from you or his mother?"

"You hang with Dominic and you call *that* smartass?"

Garrett walked to sink to wash his hands and the cutting board. He laughed and shook his head. "Got me there. Dom does smartass well." He looked over his shoulder. "He likes you a lot."

"You get that from him yelling too?"

Garrett's grin was a flash of pretty, white teeth in his dark skin. "I get that from how he's been talking about you for a very long time. Never would tell any of us who it was, but he hasn't hooked up with anyone in a long time."

"I doubt he'd appreciate you telling me that." Nevertheless, that information had his chest warming. He had to bite back a smile.

"Oh, he'll kick my ass. I just want to make sure you know he's not just in this for a good time. How about you?"

"Are you asking about my intentions toward your friend?"

Garrett shrugged, his black Ward Security polo tightening on his shoulders. He wasn't as big as some of the other bodyguards Abe had seen, but he looked to have that whipcord strength in his body—just like Dom. He probably had some kind of martial arts specialty, too. Garrett walked to another window. "He's a good guy I wouldn't want to see get hurt."

"My intentions are honorable, Garrett."

He stared at Abe a long time before slowly nodding. His cell rang and he answered as he walked out of the kitchen.

Abe stirred the beef and onions, his stomach grumbling again at the smell. Garrett had been busy and had already filled a bowl with the different spices he'd lined up behind it. They'd bought corn chips, cheese, and sour cream, so he set that out as he waited for the beef to turn brown. When they'd picked up their supplies, they'd agreed not to do the typical Cincinnati-style chili, though Dom made sure to loudly work the phrase "three-way" into their conversation all through the store.

Garrett came back into the kitchen. "That was Rowe. They haven't found James, so he's sending someone else to watch from the street tonight."

"He's taking Dom's safety seriously. Good."

"Rowe is crazy about Dom. We all are. He's a really great guy, and it sounds like he's had a shitty past. We'd like to make sure he has a great future."

Abe raised his eyebrows and pulled the pan off the stove to drain the grease. "You don't have to keep warning me off, Papa Bear." He put the pot back and added the spices and tomato sauce. "We probably should have picked up pasta for this."

Garrett shook his head, grimacing. "I grew up with Fritos and cheese."

"Don't let folks hear you say that."

"Trust me, I learned that lesson fast. Chili is serious business around here. But with spaghetti? Yeah, no." Garrett lifted the lid and sniffed. "I do like this recipe, though."

"This should really cook a few hours." Abe pulled out his phone. "We got time. It feels so much later than it actually is."

"Days like today do that." Garrett put a lid on the pot. "Why don't you quiet that loud belly with a quick sandwich, then go up and keep our sleeping friend company? You keep looking at the stairs, so I think you want to be there. We can let this simmer?"

"Good idea." Abe quickly made himself a ham sandwich and then a second one for Dom. Grabbing two bottles of water, Abe nodded at Garrett and climbed back up the stairs.

He found Dom passed out on his back, his head lolling half off the pillow. He hadn't even taken the time to put on the T-shirt still half-balled-up in his hand. Abe set the plate down on the nightstand and slowly worked to get Dom's head back on the center, careful to keep it turned so the back of it, and his cheek, stayed clear.

Green eyes opened sleepily, then focused quickly. "Everything okay?"

"Yeah," Abe said, voice gruff and low. "Sorry. I didn't mean to wake you. You've only been asleep about half an hour."

"I'm the king of power naps—it was all I needed."

"Oh yeah, then why is your voice slurred?"

"Drunk on love." Dark red lashes batted at him.

Abe rolled his eyes, but his belly did a little, giddy flip-flop. He was going to love spending his life with this man. "Sit up and have your sandwich."

But Dom didn't move, other than to scoot closer to Abe, who sat on the edge of the bed. "So Garrett is downstairs and let me guess, someone will sooner or later be lurking outside?"

"Lurking?"

"If it's Royce, it's lurking. Have you paid any attention to the man at all? He's got lurking down to an art." He sniffed the air. "Smells like you guys got dinner cooking. Thanks. I didn't mean to crash."

"Eventful fucking day."

"True, that." Dom sighed and closed his eyes. "Are you taking off those clothes and getting into this bed or what?"

"Are you again trying to figure out if I'm up for some kind of sex?" Abe repeated Dom's words from earlier. "You're insatiable!"

"Are you complaining?"

"Fuck, no."

"Because I can't seem to keep my hands off you." He proved the point by stroking his hands up Abe's arms. "God, I love your arms."

"Pretty attached to yours, too."

He flexed one, making Abe laugh and lean over to press their lips together. He touched his tongue to Dom's upper lip. He'd noticed whenever his tongue came out to play, Dom started to make the most interesting noises. He licked his bottom lip, then kissed the sexy scruff on his chin. He should have never waited so long to be with a man, because this was more awesome than he'd imagined.

Of course, that could be because his chemistry with Dom was off-the-charts hot.

The kisses grew hotter and Abe pulled back, worried about hurting Dom's cheek.

Dom merely smiled like he knew what Abe was thinking. "How long do we have until dinner with Garrett?"

"Nearly two hours," Abe murmured, kissing his jaw again before pulling back to stand and take off his clothes. "Plenty of time for you to fuck me."

Dom sat up "Really?" He glanced at the door Abe had both shut and locked because he'd been hoping Dom would be awake.

"Is that something you like to do?" he asked. "I know some men have preferences."

Dom lifted one eyebrow and a wicked smirk twisted his lips. "Been reading up, have you?"

He grinned. "Reading, watching—which is your fault because of all the damn porn. But mostly reading. I know there are some men who don't like anal sex at all, too."

"Well, we know I like it. But are you sure you will? I'm cool with anything as long as I get to feel your skin against me and smell you... and taste you."

"Just plain easy, eh?" Abe lay down on his back and pulled Dom over on top of him. "Kick off your pants."

"In a hurry, are you? No foreplay? Because you might as well learn now that I like-a the foreplay, too."

"You *like-a* the everything."

"Again the man speaks the truth." Dom braced on his side and kicked his pants off, then rolled on top of Abe.

"You didn't answer if fucking me is something you want to do," Abe murmured into his neck.

"Very much." Dom ground down against him. "I don't mind doing it the way we did last time either."

"Why don't you think I'd want to?"

Dom shrugged. "Having Garrett downstairs may make you feel self-conscious."

"Does it you?"

"Hell, no. But I am going to work to keep quieter this time. Knowing him, he'd record me and I'd walk into the office one day to hear it over the intercom."

"Would he really do that?"

Dom started laughing and he came down for a kiss. "Your expression is so horrified. Damn, you're fun. No, he wouldn't do that. I've spent too much time around Rowe and Noah, because those two are trouble."

But Abe was hardly paying attention at that point because Dom's dick kept rubbing against his stomach, and it was leaving a trail of precum that was making his thoughts scatter. He felt so good and smelled even better. "How's your head?"

"Fine."

"How's your face?"

Dom sighed. "I took a pain pill. Again, I'm up for—"

Abe cut him off with a kiss that started deep and just stayed there. He explored the other man's mouth thoroughly, chasing every trace of Dom he could find, though still careful anywhere around his left cheek.

Dom started groaning and rubbing harder against him. Abe realized he really did want to feel Dom moving inside of him like that. So, he pulled Dom back from his mouth and whispered. "I put condoms and lube in that drawer while you were getting the water going for the shower." He pointed. Abe had grabbed some supplies at the grocery store while Dom had gone in search of cookies. He didn't know if Dom had seen the purchase, but he was damn sure Garrett did.

Dom stared down at him for several, long moments and that connection he felt with the man snapped between them. Fuck, it was like only the two of them existed, and he couldn't wait for all the good stuff that was going to come.

"I really do want you like that," Abe whispered. "You're just going to have to go slow and easy this time around. Think you can do that?"

Dom groaned and dropped his forehead on the pillow beside Abe.

Abe turned and kissed his ear. "What?"

"Slow and easy coming out of your mouth is so fucking hot. Give me a minute. I'm thinking of gross things to back off the orgasm you just about yanked out of me too early."

Chuckling, Abe reached down and grabbed both globes of Dom's ass and started a slow hip-grind against him that had him seeing stars. "Slow and easy like this. I want your dick inside me and this gorgeous ass slowly flexing as you push and pull."

"Oh God, you're making it worse!" Dom rolled his hips against Abe, then carefully moved off him. He moved to stand beside the bed, chest heaving and sweaty as he stared down at Abe. He leaned over the bed and trailed his fingers on the glistening hair around Abe's navel, then bent farther and latched on to his nipple. Abe clamped a hand over his mouth to stop the wail that threatened to erupt, but his body bowed off the bed. He dropped his hand. "Grab the condom. Please."

"Shit. Don't beg. I'm just gonna stand here and shoot on you now, 'kay?"

"Don't you dare. I saw your face when I was fucking you. I want to feel like that. Want to feel you moving inside me."

"That's it." Dom stomped into the bathroom and shut the door, his voice coming through the door. "Snails. Trash. This beached whale I saw as a kid."

"That's just sad!" Abe yelled. "Get out here. Be a man."

The door opened, horror etched clearly on Dom's face. "You did not just yell that with my friend downstairs."

Abe merely grinned and crooked his finger.

Dom shook his head and approached the bed, his cock still hard and jutting out in front of his body. He got the condom and lube out of the drawer and climbed onto the bed. Then he just grinned at Abe.

"I've never laughed so much during sex in my life."

"Sex is supposed to be fun." He leaned over Abe. "And sweaty." He kissed the corner of his lips. "And dirty." He kissed the other corner. "And hot." He stuck his tongue in Abe's mouth, who grasped on to it and sucked.

Condom and lube forgotten on the bed, they wrestled and kissed and yes, laughed a few more times, but the passion flamed so hot, the laughter faded fast each time it erupted. When Dom lubed his fingers and began tracing Abe's hole, he was so turned-on, so amped up, he felt like his skin would just melt right off. He bumped his hips up, urging Dom to put a finger inside him, but Dom just shushed him with this long, sexy noise and took his sweet time.

He played, getting Abe used to the feeling of being stretched and yeah, it did sting some, but it also felt good—especially when Dom took his dick into his mouth while slowly sliding one of his long fingers up the front wall. When he crooked his finger, Abe's legs fell open and he moaned.

Then he thought about turning on music because there was no way he was going to be able to stay quiet through this. When Dom used two fingers and began fucking him with them, he held his breath, sure that it couldn't get any better than that.

But it did.

"This," Dom whispered. "Is my dactylion."

"Your huh? What?" Abe's brain could barely function.

Dom brushed one of his fingers over Abe's prostate. "The tip of my middle finger is called my dactylion."

"Dom, I can barely remember the definition of finger right now."

Dom snorted and moved his *dactylion* on Abe's spot until he was seeing nothing but stars. "Turn over," Dom whispered. "In fact, lie on your side."

Abe did and Dom came up behind him, making him shiver with excitement. His warm flesh plastered to the back of Abe, his dick rubbing slowly along his crease, his sweaty chest sliding against his back. "I think you're going to have to gag me. Or you're going to get hell from your friend down there."

"I'd forgotten he was even down there." Hot breath brushed over his neck. "You take me away from everything. When I'm with you, I only see you."

Abe turned his head and met green eyes, and he knew again this was no fling. He could see the truth of forever in Dom's gaze as well. Dom came up to kiss him softly. "You ready for me?" he whispered into his mouth.

"Yes."

And then Dom was entering his body. Letting Abe get used to him in slow increments. Again, Abe found himself holding his breath. It felt different, and his hard-on lagged a bit, but Dom felt so good against his back and his breath on Abe's shoulder made him shiver, and he loved the strong hand splayed over his belly as the man held him.

He liked this. He liked it a lot.

And once his body adjusted to the invasion, he found "a lot" didn't come close to the right description. He began moving with him and he reached back to touch Dom's hair, remembering the head wound at the last moment. So he reached down and back, clasping Dom's hip and the feel of those muscles moving under his skin made his cock surge back to life so hard, it started to ache. He wanted to grab it but didn't want to let go of Dom, especially when his hips started moving faster and he made these hot grunting noises.

"Oh fuck, I like this," he breathed.

"Thank God, because I think I want to live in here." He groaned and punched his hips again, still being careful, but obviously enjoying himself.

Abe couldn't stand it and he grabbed hold of his dick and began to stroke, not even close to the same rhythm as Dom, and he didn't give a shit because everything, all of it, felt so damn good.

He wanted Dom to live in there.

He had just enough time to smile with that thought before his orgasm slammed into him without warning. Dom hit his prostate right then, and he shot in spurts every time it was hit. He was pretty sure he was going to lose his ever-loving fucking mind.

Abe turned and bit his pillow as he just kept spilling all over the bed.

"Jesus, Abe. Shit. Shit. Shit." Dom chanted faster as his hips stuttered a couple of times; then his teeth clamped down on Abe's shoulder and Dom moaned long and hard into his skin.

Moments passed with them breathing hard.

"You okay? Abe?"

"Ghhhhhhhhghhghhghghghg."

Laughing, Dom laid his sweaty forehead against the back of Abe's neck. "Like I said before. We found something we're really good at."

Abe moved his face so that it was no longer smashed into the pillow and huffed a laugh. "We get any better and it's gonna kill me."

"Mmm...can't let that happen," Dom said, kissing along his neck and down his shoulder. "I'm hoping we get to spend a lot of time doing this in the future."

Abe's eyes slid shut and he smiled. "Lots and lots of time," he murmured.

Dom shifted behind him and Abe could feel him carefully withdrawing from his body. Abe winced. He was definitely going to be a little sore later, but he had no regrets. He could easily understand Dom's expression of pure bliss when Abe had fucked him. Staying on his side, Abe watched as Dom walked to the bathroom to dispose of the condom. The water came on and a minute later, Dom returned with a damp washcloth and a hand towel.

"We could jump back in the shower?" Dom said as he held out the washcloth.

"Later. I need to stretch out and eat that sandwich you made me completely forget about."

Dom grinned as he jumped back onto the bed and picked up the plate of sandwiches. Abe finished cleaning up, dropping both the washcloth and towel on the floor, and sat up against the pillows. He stomach growled loudly at the sight of the sandwich, angry at him for choosing sex over food, but Abe didn't give a damn. He was happy to choose Dom first every time.

A low moan rippled from Dom around a mouthful of ham and bread. "You make a mean sammich, Abe," he said after swallowing.

"Not as good as those sandwiches we had with Trent, but it'll fill the hole until the chili is ready," Abe conceded.

"Those were damn good sandwiches," Dom agreed with a nod. "I need to text Trent. Get him to tell me the place he ordered them from. And the name of that mustard again. Good stuff."

Abe took another bite of his sandwich to hide his smirk. Only Dom would think to text a freaking A-list celebrity for the name of a mustard and a sandwich shop. It really was no surprise that he'd fallen so hard for this man. He hadn't stood a chance.

The mention of Trent got Abe's mind turning to an idea he had earlier. Something more than a little crazy and a whole hell of a lot dangerous. Probably stupid too. And a little illegal. But it could mean freeing Dom of his brother once and for all.

"You know that idea I had percolating in my brain?" Abe hesitantly started. "You think Trent would be up for giving us a hand?"

Dom's hand stopped in midair as he was about to place the last bite of sandwich into his open mouth. Muscles tensed for a second before Dom lowered his hand and looked at him. "Actor Trent?"

"Yes."

"Is your idea crazy and dangerous?"

"Yes."

Dom stared at him for a second before nodding, his face breaking out in a wide grin. "Then yes, I think he would. He seemed a little jealous of my effective defenestration of his stalker and is looking for a little real-life action."

Abe looked down at the last couple of bites of his sandwich, no longer feeling quite so hungry. "Don't worry. I think my idea is gonna have plenty of action."

CHAPTER SIXTEEN

Abe wanted to smack himself as he walked through Washington Park in the waning sunlight three days later. The film crew that had set up in the park the previous week was now gone, and the green space was largely back to its usual beauty. There were a few families crossing the area, but it was mostly adults strolling through, on their way to the restaurants and bars that filled Over-the-Rhine. His pulse was racing, and a cold sweat had broken out across his arms as he slowed his pace the closer he got to the chosen meeting spot.

After leaving Dom at Royce's, he'd stopped by his house and quickly changed clothes before driving to downtown Cincinnati. The entire time, he had at least one person from Ward Security murmuring in his ear. By the time he left his house, he'd picked up a tail. It wasn't the same car he'd spotted the one day he'd met Shane and Quinn for lunch. This was an SUV with the windows tinted so dark he couldn't see the occupants. He didn't know if James was in that SUV, but he was counting on the fact that James knew exactly where to find him now.

"Abe! Hey Abe!" called a voice that was so close to being Dom's.

Close, but the difference was like needles in his ears. That voice was a little rougher, a little sharper in its edge. It didn't carry the love he could feel emanating from Dom, and it was all he could do not to flinch.

"That is not me, sexy," Dom whispered to him through the tiny earwig buried deep in his ear canal. He wanted to reassure Dom that he wasn't fooled. That the voice would never fool him, but he couldn't risk it. Instead, he plastered a smile on his face and turned toward the man who had Dom's face.

"There you are!" he called back, throwing his hands up. "I was beginning to think you'd forgotten." As James approached, he noted a little hitch in his step as if he was slightly thrown by Abe's words, but it never showed on his face.

As much as it killed him, Abe had to admit that there was a startling similarity between Dom and James. They had the same build, the same walk, the same wide grin, but the most glaring difference was in their eyes. They might have the same shade of green, but there was nothing warm and gentle in James's eyes. Only malice and cold calculation. This man he would never mistake for Dom, but for the next hour, he had to pretend if he was ever going to save Dom's life and possibly even his own.

"Sorry, Abe. Traffic was worse than I'd expected," James said with a little shrug. "Unfortunately, I just got a call from the office."

"Rowe?"

"Yeah, um...I need to head in to help with something, and I was wondering if you'd come with me and then we could go out."

"But—"

James's hand clamped down on Abe's upper arm as he started to argue. The man leaned forward for a kiss, and Abe fought not to clench up. He had to act natural. If he didn't kiss James, then the man would know that he was faking. He could do this for Dom.

Just before James's lips reached his, a blessedly familiar voice cried out.

"Dom! Abe!"

Abe's head snapped up to see Trent briskly walking across the park toward them. He was dressed in a pair of dark jeans that nicely accentuated his powerful legs and a loose shirt. A ballcap was pulled low and a pair of dark sunglasses helped to hide his face. The damn actor had absolutely perfect timing.

"Hey!" Abe said, catching himself before he could shout out Trent's name. They were still in a very public place, and they couldn't risk drawing a mob of fans to the man. But the sudden distraction was enough for James to loosen his hold on Abe's arm, so he could pull away.

"Are you guys ready for a great dinner and a little dancing?" Trent asked when he was standing next to Abe. Trent pulled off his sunglasses, giving James a good view of his face.

"Holy shit! Trent Elrige!" James said on a gasp.

Abe winced, but Trent just gave a sarcastic laugh, covering up James's unfortunate lapse. "Oh, ha ha, Dom. Don't start that shit again after everything we've been through. You're the one who called me about tonight."

Abe nearly snorted. This acting shit was harder than he'd expected, but Trent...Trent was amazing. He couldn't remember if the man had won an Oscar yet, but he'd definitely deserve one by the end of the night for the way he was flawlessly ad-libbing.

"Of course," James quickly said. "I just thought you'd feel more at ease if someone was acting like an adoring fan."

Trent slipped his glasses back on and smirked. "Nah. I can enjoy one night as just a normal guy. No fans, please. Just friends."

"Nothing but friends here," James quickly said.

With that, Abe did roll his eyes, though he was facing Trent so James couldn't see it. If this guy was an expert con artist, then he was thrown off his game with the presence of Trent. Not that Abe could really blame him. If he hadn't had dinner with Trent already, he'd probably be stumbling as much as James or worse.

"Dom was just telling me that he's been called into the office," Abe said.

Trent winced. "Oh, that sucks. Is it a new job?"

"No, just some paperwork." He paused and his grin grew. "But you both could come with me before we go out to dinner. Trent, you could check out where all the bodyguards train and meet. That could be useful for a future role, right?"

"Sure, I'd love to see Ward Security. I've heard so much about it," Trent easily agreed.

Abe chanced a glance over at James and the man was practically bouncing in his excitement. And why wouldn't he be? Not only did he have Abe in his clutches, which would break his brother as he wanted, but he also had his hands on one of the hottest actors in Hollywood. This had to be a freaking dream come true for the con artist.

"Get ready," Dom whispered in his ear, and some of the tension eased from his shoulders. He didn't know where Dom was, but he was watching over him, keeping him safe. And even though he was technically in James's clutches, Abe still felt safe.

Yeah, get ready, he thought, *for a day in the life of Dominic fucking Walsh.*

"Trent Elrige! I'm gonna fucking kill you!"

"What the fuck?" James muttered as they all turned to stare at the large man in a dark hoodie pulled up to obscure his face. He looked like a mountain.

"How many stalkers do you have?" Abe said, backpedaling into James.

"Too many," Trent grumbled.

The enormous man pulled a gun from behind his back and started to wave it in their direction. Some people screamed and scattered in various directions. Abe tried not to wince and mentally prayed that they had a couple of minutes before someone called the cops. Abe had met Sven Larsen only once before, but he was a truly frightening figure without a gun. He certainly didn't want the bodyguard to go to jail for brandishing a weapon in public.

"Jesus!" James shouted. Abe saw him start to reach behind him for what he was sure was a gun. He couldn't let him pull a gun on the other man. The "stalker" was a Ward Security employee, and he couldn't risk James hurting him.

"No, there are too many people here. Someone could get hurt," Abe argued.

James looked at him for a second like he'd lost his mind. Yeah, not the best argument when someone was barreling down on them with a weapon, but it was all he could think of.

"There!" Trent pointed toward a black BMW sedan parked nearby. "That's my car with my driver. Run! Hurry!" As he shouted, Trent gave James two hard pushes, knocking him off balance so that he was moving toward the car, if only to steady himself. Abe started running ahead of them, certain that James would follow to keep him under his control.

"Trent! I'm going to get you! You can't escape me, Trent!" the stalker continued to shout, following after them.

Abe reached the car first. Jerking open the rear door, he dove inside. He kept scooting until he was seated behind the driver. A pair of bright blue eyes met his in the rearview mirror and winked at him. The man's normally curly brownish-blond hair was pulled tightly back at the nape of his neck and he was dressed in a dark suit, but there was no mistaking Noah Keegan. Abe had been lucky enough to meet Noah when he'd popped by Ward Security once before. When they'd cooked up this scheme, Rowe had assured him that he'd get his guy with the gun off the street before the cops arrived and that his best driver would be behind the wheel. He'd just never expected it to be Rowe's own boyfriend.

But there was no time to say anything. The front door was thrown open, and Trent tumbled inside while James followed Abe into the rear. Doors slammed shut.

"Drive!" Trent shouted.

Noah stomped on the gas and the car leaped forward in a squeal of tires and the sharp smell of rubber on asphalt. They were thrown back in their seats as the BMW darted into traffic. As soon as they could move, they glanced behind them to see the giant man leap into an SUV and start after them.

"I need you to lose that man, Drew," Trent instructed. "He's trying to kill us."

"Yes, sir," Noah replied in a low, steady voice as if it was a command he heard frequently from his clients.

The engine roared and the BMW powered down Race Street toward the heart of downtown, and then the car turned left twice, heading north again. They went a few more blocks before Noah made another left, taking them closer to the interstate highway. Abe knew that Quinn was in Noah's ear, directing him away from any cops that might be in the area, while Gidget and Cole were focused on keeping the lights changing in their favor.

"Who the hell is this guy?" James snarled as he looked over his shoulder again toward the SUV that was still following them.

"Another crazy stalker," Trent said with a blasé tone, as if this happened to him every day.

"I thought I took care of your stalker."

Trent scoffed and adjusted his seat belt. Abe did the same, while James remained without his. Abe wasn't going to tell the man to buckle up. Let him take the chance of going through the windshield.

"I have more than one stalker," Trent said.

"Maybe we should call the cops," Abe offered.

"No cops!" James shouted. He took a deep breath and continued in a normal voice. "I'm sure that Trent's driver can lose this asshole. When we are safe, then we can discuss calling the police."

"Sounds like a good plan to me," Trent said,

Abe looked out the rear window and frowned. The stalker SUV was still there, but behind it, he spotted the same SUV that had followed him from his house. It had to be the rest of James's crew. That was to be expected.

Glancing up again, he saw Noah meet his gaze and give a quick nod. They made another left, and the light changed directly behind them. Noah zipped up and down several side streets, leading them farther and farther away from downtown Cincinnati, into an industrial section filled with railyards and old warehouses. The road was rutted and bumpy, but Noah didn't slow the car.

"Where the hell are we? Where are you taking us?" James demanded. He leaned forward, glaring out the windshield and then twisting around in his seat to glower out the back window. The stalker SUV, as well as the tinted SUV, were both missing.

"A special meeting zone we pre-arranged when I arrived in the city," Trent replied. "Another car is going to be waiting for us there. We'll switch cars and then we can head back to my hotel or out for the evening. The stalker won't be looking for the new car."

"No, we can't do that," James cried.

"Oh, that's right. You have to go back to Ward Security," Abe said.

"Of course!" Trent said. He shifted in his seat to look into the rear at Abe and James. "When we get the new car, we can head straight to Ward."

James shook his head, looking utterly lost for a second. "No, I...I need my car. The paperwork Rowe needs, it's in my car."

"Oh, okay. When we meet up with the new driver, then we'll head back and switch to your car. From there, we can go to Ward. It'll be easier to report the stalker from there," Trent easily said.

"Yeah...yeah, that'll work," James murmured, his voice so low, he was almost talking to himself.

Abe's stomach nervously churned and bubbled. The rough ride didn't help to settle his stomach or slow his pulse. So far, everything was going exactly as they had planned, but they were quickly nearing their final destination, and that was where everything could blow up in their faces. Abe was all too aware of the gun that was still hidden somewhere on James's person. He wanted to get that away from James, but he'd yet to think of a way to get it that wouldn't raise James's suspicions. That damn weapon was one of the few things they couldn't control, and it gave James the power to end a lot of innocent lives.

He strained to hear anything other than the roar of the car engine and the frantic beating of his own heart, but there was no one talking to him over his earpiece. No updates. No reassuring words. They'd warned him that contact would be kept to a minimum so as not to risk catching James's attention, but even with Noah in the car with them, Abe was starting to feel very alone and out of his element. It amazed him that Dom could do such a dangerous job and keep such a positive attitude the entire time.

When Abe's fiftieth birthday had started to creep closer and he started to long for a little more excitement and adventure, this had definitely not crossed his mind. Skydiving...that would have been safer. Maybe swimming with sharks. A crash course in wrestling alligators. Not this. But Dom was worth it.

"Sir, I'm sorry," Noah started in a low voice.

"What's wrong, Drew?" Trent straightened in his seat and looked around.

"The SUV that was following us has returned," Noah said.

"Fuck!" Trent snarled. They all looked out the rearview mirror to see the SUV driven by the stalker was behind them again. But the tinted SUV carrying James's crew was missing. Abe didn't know if they were simply lost or if Ward's people had intercepted them. Either way, it was one less thing to worry about for now.

"What the fuck!" James swore beside him in stunned confusion.

"Here! Go in here and see if we can lose him among the warehouses," Trent directed, pointing off to his right.

Noah jerked the wheel and the car jumped the curb, darting through an opening in a sagging chain link fence. The parking lot was filled with fractured concrete and weeds growing up through the cracks. The warehouses had their windows darkened and partially boarded up. A For Sale sign was nailed to the side of one of the buildings. It looked like they were the only ones in the place. Perfect.

"Brace!" warned a low voice in his ear. Possibly Rowe's.

Abe grasped the door handle and tightened his seat belt a second before Noah swore and violently jerked the wheel. There was a horrendous scraping noise as something rubbed against the undercarriage of the car. It helped to significantly slow them down, but not as much as the telephone pole. The BMW came to a painful halt as the front hit the pole and stopped. Airbags exploded around them, and Abe sat in dazed silence for a second. There was an ache in his bones from the impact, but he knew he wasn't feeling the worst of it yet. That would come later when the adrenaline subsided.

Blinking a couple of times, Abe watched as Trent released his seat belt and reached over to Noah, who was lying against the steering wheel, the airbag deflating quickly beneath him.

"Oh God," Trent moaned. "Drew is dead. He's dead."

Abe couldn't help the skip of his heart. Was he really dead? Or was Trent still acting? The impact hadn't felt that hard, but it was enough to spiderweb the windshield. It looked like there was blood running down along the white airbag. Was Noah...dead? Had his plan killed Rowe's lover?

"He's fine, Abe," Rowe calmly said in his ear. "He gave the signal."

A whimper of relief slipped from Abe's lump-clogged throat, but he didn't care. The noise could just have easily been mistaken for pain and horror. He was ready for this to be over, but he had one more part to play.

"We have to go," James said. "The stalker is still out there."

Abe nodded slowly, unbuckling his seat belt. He pushed open his car door and slid out. His body protested the movement, but he gritted his teeth and stood. He was going to need some great painkillers and a massage if he managed to survive this bullshit.

Running his hand along the side of the car to help keep his balance, Abe moved to the trunk with Trent and James. He glanced around and there was no one about...except for the SUV and the giant man stepping out of it.

"The warehouse!" Trent said, pointing to the closest warehouse with the open rear door. "We can hide in there and call the cops."

James stared at it and nodded. He looked utterly dazed and

confounded by the events unfolding around him. Abe almost felt pity for the bastard. He'd undoubtedly thought he'd just be kidnapping an old man right out from under Dom's nose. Not get taken on a wild adventure.

"Trent Elrige!" the stalker shouted. He came around the side of his SUV and lifted his gun, pointing it at Trent. "You're fucking dead, asshole!"

"Hey man," Trent said. He lifted his empty hands, holding them out to the side. "I don't know what I've done to upset you, but I'm sure we can talk about it. Figure this out calmly." He took a couple of steps so that he was standing right next to Abe while James was behind them both.

The gun in the stalker's hand went off three times. Trent's body twisted and jerked as blood jumped from his chest and he collapsed to the ground. The stalker then pointed the gun at Abe, and the entire world slowed down to a crawl. He sucked in a ragged breath. Never had he thought that he'd stare down the barrel of a gun. There was no sound, but there was an explosion from the end of the weapon. And then three sharp, painful bursts thudded against his chest. He gasped and let his body go limp as he fell forward.

The squibs exploded against his chest in the little make-shift vest they'd placed on him under his button-down shirt, which was now ruined. At least it wasn't his favorite. His chest felt like someone had hit him with a hammer, and he swore he could smell burned chest hair, but he ignored it, trying to remember the instructions Trent had given him on playing dead. Be still. Let your entire body go completely loose.

Gravel dug into his cheek and the fake blood was seeping through his shirt, chilling his skin. More shots were fired. This time from James's direction and Abe prayed for the fake stalker. He was relieved when he heard the squeal of tires as the SUV peeled out of the empty parking lot.

There was a scrabble of feet on the broken pavement and then a hand on his shoulder, tilting him slightly upright. Abe struggled to keep his gaze unfocused.

"Run, Dom!" he choked out. "Call for help." He gave a thick, phlegmy cough. "Run."

"Yeah, help," James mumbled, releasing Abe to flop back down on the sun-warmed pavement. There were more footsteps, but this time they were running away from the car...toward the warehouse.

Closing his eyes, Abe chanced a deep, shaky breath. The overwhelming need to both laugh and cry rose up inside of him at the same time. He'd come up with this insane plan and somehow, he'd managed to survive it. There was just one more dangerous part, and there was nothing he could do to help Dom from this point on.

"Hey, Abe."

"Yeah, Trent," he replied, still lying facedown on the pavement.

"This is a normal day for Dom?"

"Yep."

"Fuck...I need a damn vacation after this."

"Yeah, me too." Taking a deep breath, he whispered, "He's all yours, Dom. Be safe."

CHAPTER SEVENTEEN

Dom waited in the shadows, sweat running down the side of his face in the stifling hot warehouse. He held close Abe's admonishment to be safe. It was not his priority, but for Abe, he would try. They were not finished, not by a long shot. He wanted everything that a relationship offered when it came to Abe. He wanted the arguments and the tense moments of fear as much as he wanted years of laughter and joy. He wanted to wake up beside Abe and plan their day while lying in bed.

But first he had to deal with James.

His brother had threatened Abe, threatened the family that he built with Ward Security. Threatened the fucking life that he'd finally gotten for himself after years of struggle. It couldn't continue.

James might be all that was left of his blood relatives, but it carried no weight when it came to the lives of the people that he loved.

When Abe had described his plan, he was sure that his lover had absolutely lost his mind, but then they wrangled in Rowe and Trent. They all rallied together to help Dom. To confuse and distract James until he ran straight into Dom's clutches.

"We've got Abe and Trent in sight with Noah. We'll have them in two minutes," Rowe relayed in the earwig he was wearing.

"Got it."

"Don't be stupid, Dom," Rowe said in a low, firm voice. "We need you back safe and sound too."

Dom grunted. He wasn't planning to be stupid, but there were a few choice words he wanted to say to his brother before this was finally over.

Heavy footsteps pounded on the pavement and echoed off the high walls and ceilings in the empty, two-story warehouse. Dom watched from his perch atop of a pair of crates in the shadows as his brother ran into the warehouse and slammed the door shut behind him. He continued to move into the room, twisting to the left and then right as if searching for some unseen assailant. Harsh, broken breaths filled the relative silence, and James frantically ran his hand through his hair.

"Fuck!" he swore softly, and then a second time, louder. Loud enough to disturb the doves from where they were roosting up in the steel rafters. Reaching into his back pocket, he pulled out his cell phone. After tapping a couple of buttons, he held it up to his ear while he paced in the center of the room. He swore again after a few seconds and lowered the phone. He tried again…and again.

"What the fuck, Slaney? Where are you?" he snarled. He tried again but still got no answer. He started to throw his phone but caught himself at the last second and shoved it into his back pocket again.

"Trouble?" Dom called out.

James spun around, whipping out the gun he had concealed in a holster at his back. "John?" He pointed it in the general area where Dom was but had yet to actually spot him.

Dom let the name slide without comment as he jumped down from his perch. He wasn't worried about the gun, yet. And he'd learned from his past mistakes when it came to James, bringing his own to this fight.

"Can't reach your crew?" he continued.

The confusion twisting up James's features cleared and was replaced by rage. "What did you do? Where the fuck is Slaney and the rest of my pack?" He stomped toward Dom, the gun pointed right at his face, and Dom just smiled at him.

"Right now, they would be in police custody. They should be matching your people's prints to The Joint and the weapon that killed the bar owner. I wouldn't be surprised if there were a few other unsolved crimes around the area that could be tied back to your pack."

"Fuck off! You think you've won, but you ain't won shit. Your boyfriend is dead. You're going to be blamed for the death of Trent Elrige. You're going to lose everything. I can create another pack. Nothing is going to stop me."

Dom chuckled at his brother, his grin growing wide. "Abe's dead? Trent's dead?" He shook his head. "Sounds like you had a rough day pretending to be me."

James stared at him, the confusion returning. The gun in his hand slowly lowered back to his side and he took an unsteady step backward. "What? How?"

"You mean, how did I know that Abe, who was completely off the grid for three days, just suddenly ran back to his house, the one place your people were sure to be watching? And then you just happen to catch him out in the open in Washington Park. Where you just so happen to meet up with a freaking movie star?"

"Of course, you expected me to follow Abe," James snapped, but his voice lacked the same mocking strength and conviction he'd had just a few minutes earlier. He waved the gun widely as he spoke. "I told you I was going to get Abe. He was your weakness."

"Abe is my strength," Dom corrected in a hard, cold voice. He slowly paced, walking around James so that he was forced to turn in a tight circle if he wanted to keep Dom in view. "But how could you pass up the chance to grab both Abe and a movie star? That was a once in a lifetime opportunity, wasn't it?"

"I don't..." James started to say, but his voice trailed off.

"But then Trent had a stalker who chased you to Trent's nearby car. That had to have been a wild ride through the city. Must have been hard for your people to keep up. There was always the chance that you'd lose your backup to a red light and heavy downtown traffic."

"You!" he gasped.

"Ward Security intercepted your crew, disabled them for the cops, while you continued on to here. A fake car accident. Blanks and some exploding squibs with fake blood put both Trent and Abe out of your reach. And you...you're alone, confused, and desperate for escape and ran straight in here after Trent mentioned it."

"You-you fucking conned me," James stammered in shock.

"Dad taught us both," Dom sneered. "You think I forgot all that shit? Forgot what it takes to get a person to believe and do exactly what you want them to? You think you're smarter than everyone, but yeah, I conned you."

James backpedaled away from Dom. His sweat-covered face was pale in the light coming through the dirty windows of the warehouse. He shook his head once, mouthing the word *no*. Dom braced himself, muscles bunched and ready to strike if James decided to lift the gun again. There were several feet between them, but he was sure that he could cross the distance in time to knock the gun away.

And then James started laughing. Deep, loud belly laughs. He dropped the gun to his side, hanging loose from just a few fingers. He held his stomach with his free hand and laughed wildly. When his gaze returned to Dom, he shook his head as he continued to chortle. "Dad was wrong about you. He was fucking wrong," he said when he could drag in a deep breath. Dom remained cautious, not sure what his brother was talking about.

"He said you didn't have what it takes to be a wolf. He said that you were always too soft, too worried about the marks." James snorted. "Said you were nothing more than a weak sheep pretending to be a wolf. He was glad you were dead."

Dom clenched his teeth but said nothing. There was no love lost between himself and his father. He couldn't say that he was surprised by his father's comments, and they certainly didn't hurt like they should have.

Staring down at the gun in his hand, James gave a little smirk and returned his sparkling green eyes up to Dom. "This con...your greatest con ever...proves to me that I was justified in killing the old bastard. He couldn't talk about you like that. Talk about us like that. You're not a sheep. You're a killer wolf just like me." Unexpectedly, James charged him faster than Dom could react. Reaching out, James grabbed the back of Dom's head and pulled him forward until their foreheads touched. "My brother is back and he's ruthless. We're back."

Dom shoved his brother off in revulsion and backpedaled. "You cut my face. Threatened to kill my boyfriend. Threatened to kill me. How could you think that I'd want anything to do with you?"

"I had to do those things, John. In order to save you. To bring you back to me." James reached out with his empty hand, but there was no forgetting that he still held a gun in the other. "If I didn't do those things, if I hadn't pushed you, we wouldn't be standing right here, right now. You'd be dead. My crew and I would have those jeweled handbags and headed to a nice tropical vacation. But you pull this awesome con!" He threw his arms up in the air and howled, sending the chilling sound up to bounce off the ceiling and down to them again. "Seriously, a work of art. So impressed." He brought his hand to his lips and made a kissing sound. "Bravo."

"You're insane," Dom muttered, shaking his head.

"And now, we'll just slip out of town together. You shed this silly life here, and we'll get back down to business. We won't need a pack like my old one. We'll operate, just the two of us again. We'll tear the world apart. No one will ever be able to catch us."

"No! *This* is my life. I love my life. I love the people I work with and protecting good people. I love Abe Stephens. There is nothing you can say that would make me walk away from that. I've got everything I've ever wanted here."

James's expression slowly morphed from one of disbelief to rage. Dom knew he couldn't understand why Dom would choose this life over the one they'd had, but he didn't care. James started to lift the gun back toward Dom. There was no talking his way around the gun this time, which was just fine with Dom. He was done talking.

Lunging forward, Dom grabbed James's wrist, wrenching it at a key pressure point. James screamed in pain, his fingers loosening so that the gun clattered to the concrete floor. Dom kicked it, sending it skidding away from them. James took advantage of his distracted gaze, punching Dom with his free hand and snapping his head around.

Dom released James and backed up a couple of steps. He had no idea if his brother had picked up any fighting skills over the years beyond his usual street brawler style, but he knew to expect the man to fight dirty. James didn't care about fighting fair. Just winning.

With his hands balled into fists in front of his face, James stalked after Dom. They circled each other, moving into the large, open space in the center of the old warehouse. There were a few broken pallets that once held raw materials for the old mill, but the machinery had been sold off and moved out years ago. The light through the windows was waning, and soon they'd be fighting in the dark if Dom didn't settle this with James quickly.

Dom's right hand shot out, his fingers flicking. The feint wasn't intended to actually make contact, but rather to check his brother's reaction. Did he swing? Block? Retreat?

James batted Dom's hand away and took a wide swing. Not the trained response that Dom had worried about. He could work with that. Dom sent out two more flicker punches in James's line of sight, the last one flicking the tip of his nose.

A snarl of frustration rumbled in the back of James's throat. Dom almost chuckled at how easily annoyed James had become. Of course, he might also be stewing about the fact that Dom totally played him with Abe and Trent.

Dom started to lead with his right hand again. James was already reacting, his hands loosening as he prepared to bat Dom's hand away. Instead, Dom ducked low, delivering a hard blow to James's midsection, just under his ribs, with his left. He followed with a right to James's chin, knocking him stumbling backward. James quickly backpedaled, putting more space between them. Dom followed, looking to end the fight quickly.

But James caught him off guard by diving to his side and rolling back up to his feet nearly a yard away. And when he came up this time, he looked decidedly more prepared than he had when they first squared off.

"What's wrong, John?" James taunted. "Did you think I just sat on my ass when you disappeared?"

"You preferred to settle things with a gun, last I remember. Not much of a hands-on kind of guy," Dom said.

James chuckled low. "For you, I'll make an exception."

Dom wanted to charge the fucker again, but he had to play it cautiously. He didn't know his brother's moves, and he didn't know if he had any more weapons on him. This time he'd brought his own gun, but he wasn't going to pull it on a supposedly unarmed man. Besides, he really wanted to knock the shit out of his brother before the cops finally arrived. For now, he was content to keep him talking.

"Did you make the same exception when you killed our father?"

James snorted. "Is this for whatever wire or recording devices happen to be in the warehouse?"

"Just between you, me, and the birds in the ceiling."

"Pfft...whatever. Doesn't matter. I'm going to kill you, and I'll walk away because no one can tell us apart. They'll think it's James O'Brien dead on the ground regardless, and I'll just go on being Dominic Walsh. You know why? Because we look the same. We sound the same. We have the same fucking DNA."

"We're not the same person, you fucking psychopath!" Dom roared.

James took advantage of Dom's rage. Lowering his shoulder, he plowed into Dom's stomach, taking him straight to the ground. Pain exploded in Dom's back, and his breath rushed out of his lungs. James got his knees under him and attempted to straddle Dom's waist, but Dom quickly dug his heels into the concrete and rolled, putting him on top of James. The other man locked his legs around Dom's waist so that he could move into full control. Didn't matter. Andrei had given him more than enough grappling lessons over the past year. He could manage just fine.

He caught James's left hand with his right, pinning it to the ground. With his left forearm, he pummeled the bridge of James's nose again and again. He could feel it break by the third hit and then moved his aim to James's right eye. Enough hits and it would swell shut, partially blinding him.

James countered by trying to push Dom off him or swing his free hand, but Dom kept his head tucked close to his shoulder and chest so that James didn't have a clear target. But it also meant that he didn't see James snatch up a loose board from a broken pallet. The wood slammed against Dom's temple.

Falling away from James at the same time as his brother pushed him, Dom rolled to his side and back to his feet. He swayed, the darkening world a little blurry as pain splintered through his skull. He was aware of James skittering off in the opposite direction. In the same direction that James's gun had flown when Dom knocked it away.

Dom stepped away from James, blinking hard to clear his vision. He reached behind his back and pulled out the gun sitting snug in its holster at the small of his back. At the same time, he heard the telltale scrape of metal along concrete. James had found the gun.

"James," Dom said in warning. His brother had pushed to his feet several yards away and was standing with his back to Dom. His shoulders were slightly bowed in and he was breathing heavily, each gasping breath filling the quiet of the warehouse. Dom was balanced on the balls of his feet, ready to move, while still holding his gun down at his side. He would never shoot a man in the back, and he would never shoot an unarmed man. But he was pretty sure that only one of those things described James at that moment.

"It doesn't have to end like this, James," Dom started again. His voice was rough as a lump of rage and something else started to form in his throat. "You can just go back to California and forget that I exist. Go back to your life and I'll go back to mine."

"It's all or nothing, John," James whispered.

"No! No, it's not! We're brothers, dammit. *Brothers.* You're the last of my flesh and blood. Why can't we just be fucking brothers?"

"Because it's not like that with us."

"Why? Didn't you ever just want to hang out? Grab pizza. Go to a movie. Just...be brothers. None of this other shit."

James shook his head. "We were meant for bigger and better things than that." He straightened as he spoke.

"Don't, James."

"We are wolves."

"James..."

"And if you're not a part of my pack..." James swung around to face Dom, lifting the gun as he turned.

Clenching his teeth, Dom raised his gun at the same time. He pivoted his hips, turning as much of his body sideways as he could to give James less of a target. Slowly, he released a breath and squeezed the trigger. The explosion in the warehouse was enormous, deafening Dom. Both guns went off at the same time.

James flew backward and hit the ground hard. The hand holding the gun was thrown wide. One more shot was fired, but it was nowhere near Dom. James didn't make a sound. Dom patted his own chest in shock. He was unharmed. His brother's shot missed him.

Keeping his gun drawn, Dom slowly edged over to where James was lying unmoving on the concrete. There was just enough light to see the gun had fallen from James's hand and was laying a few feet away. A growing circle of blood was spreading across his chest, where Dom's bullet had gone straight through his heart. There was no breath. No movement. James's wide green eyes stared blankly up at the ceiling.

"James?" Dom croaked. His knees gave out and he collapsed to the floor next to his brother's body. With a shaking hand, he reached out and pressed his fingers along his neck. He tried again and again, angry at the trembling he couldn't control, but he couldn't find a pulse.

Oh God, he'd shot his brother. Killed him.

A broken sob escaped his throat, and he sat down hard on the cooling concrete next to his brother. Yes, James would have killed him. Tried to kill him. But Dom had never wanted this. He just wanted to be free. To be a good man.

"Dom?" Abe's voice was like a soothing balm in his ear. Dom's head jerked up and he looked around, the warehouse blurry through the tears streaking down his cheeks. But he was still alone. Abe's voice had come from the earwig he was still wearing. "Dom, baby. Please, talk to me. What happened?"

"He's gone. I killed him. He was my brother..." He pressed his hands to his eyes as the words came pouring out. He still held the damn gun like it was melded to his skin.

"I'm coming. I'll be there soon. Just hang on."

"Hurry. Please," Dom whispered. He couldn't do this without Abe. Everything hurt too much and the only thing that didn't hurt, that still made sense, was Abe.

CHAPTER EIGHTEEN

On Abe's fiftieth birthday, he woke to the acrid scent of burning candles and a warm mouth surrounding his dick. He looked down to see a naughty gleam in the beautiful green eyes looking up at him. He moaned as Dom tightened his lips and used his tongue to explore a vein, then came up to lick around the head.

Abe's eyes shut and the sheet fell off one leg as he brought them both up to better push deeper into Dom's throat. Fuck, he loved how Dom got off on that, and his boyfriend's answering groan sent a shiver racing up his spine. He opened his eyes, watching his cock disappear in Dom's mouth, and the hoarse sort of chuckle and choke that escaped him brought the eyes back to him.

"So good, Dom. I could wake like this every day."

Dom pulled off. "That could be arranged."

"Agh! Why'd you stop?"

Nuzzling into Abe's balls, his hot breath made Abe shiver as he asked, "How's my quinquagenarian doing today?"

"Let me guess—that has something to do with me turning fifty?"

Dom held up his dick and licked the tip of it. "It does. Mmmm, fifty tastes good on you."

Grasping Dom under the arms, Abe dragged him up his body and stuck out his tongue. Dom touched his to it, grinning before he slid the whole thing into Abe's mouth. He buried his fingers in Dom's hair, glad he could because the man's head had healed. He tugged on the soft hair a little and when Dom came up, he kissed the scar on his face, then his nose, which wrinkled as he laughed.

"Did you set my house on fire? Because it smells like it."

"Fifty candles are a lot." Dom sat up, straddling him, and pointed to the bedside table where he'd put a tall stack of pancakes with a mass of candles burning and melting all over them. "We'll have to ditch the top one because I got distracted by the enticing tent in the covers you'd made." He glanced over his shoulder. "The one you're still making."

Abe held his breath when Dom reached behind him and made a tugging motion before he tossed his favorite plug onto the floor. He held Abe's gaze as he backed up and slid his ass onto Abe.

The plug had left him open, so Abe slid right in to the hilt. They'd both been tested and going bare with Dom made him feel even more deeply connected to the man. And holy shit, it felt good to slide into that scorching channel. He could live there.

"Best. Birthday. Ever." His words were punctuated with thrusts of his hips. "Love the way you feel inside—so hot and tight."

"Feels like it's *my* birthday," Dom breathed as he braced those sexy-as-fuck arms on either side of Abe and went to town on his dick. Up and down he moved before rolling his hips.

Abe reached down and clutched his ass as he fucked deep into Dom's body. He couldn't take his eyes off the beautiful man doing his best to pull his brains out through his cock. Muscles rippled in his arms and shoulders, his abs doing that sexy, quivering dance as he moved his hips. All of him was so beautiful, yet the best part of him was the way he looked down at Abe, the way his eyes slid mostly shut when pleasure overtook him. He loved fully, and Abe felt like the luckiest man on Earth. "I love you so much," Abe whispered.

"Love you, too. *Agh!*" Dom sat back, sending Abe deep. He cried out again, the veins standing out in his neck. "There! Oh, it's so damn good right there. God, I love that fat cock of yours!"

Vocal Dom was always added pleasure and Abe pushed into him hard, forcing out all kinds of sexy noises, cries, and grunts. Dom suddenly clamped down on him so hard, Abe saw stars.

"I'm gonna come!"

"Yeah, baby, do it." Abe loved to watch Dom spill all over him, and he watched with greedy eyes as the man above him came apart. As always, that was enough to send Abe over with him, and he groaned long and loud as he came inside Dom.

Dom slumped over him, breathing hard into his neck, dropping a kiss every few seconds. He finally laughed and squeezed his arm around Abe's waist before looking at the bedside table. "Those cheap-ass candles burned out. And yeah, we're not eating that top one unless you were one of those kids who actually ate the little wax bottles filled with juice."

"How do you even know about those?"

"Retro Candy, how else?"

Abe rolled his eyes and hugged him close. "I love that you made me pancakes and I'll eat them, waxy or not."

"You're so easy."

"We just proved that." Abe stared into Dom's face, watching for the hints of sadness that had flitted through so often in the days after he'd taken his brother's life, glad to see none.

The police had ruled James's death self-defense, and considering nobody had known of John O'Brien's existence, James had been the one wanted for all those crimes in the past. It had been touch-and-go for a while as Abe worried Dom's past would come back to bite him in the ass. Outside of a lot of questioning, and hours spent sharing the cipher and more, the authorities had many past crimes that were now pinned on James and his crew. The police had rounded them up, thanks to a little help from Ward Security, and Abe doubted they'd see freedom for a long time.

He had a feeling Rowe and his powerful friends had a little to do with the fact that Dom wasn't in trouble for using his current identity. Hell, his birth one had never legally existed.

Dom sat up and swung his legs to the side of the bed. He gave Abe a saucy grin before sauntering naked into the master bath. He came back with a warm rag he used to clean Abe; then he stood eyeing the pancakes, with a frown crinkling his nose and brow. "We're not eating these. Good thing I saved the batter. Come on." He held out his hand. "Let's go have a very unhealthy breakfast. I want bacon, too. I picked some up on the way here last night."

"You don't have cake planned for tonight at your place, do you?"

"It's a birthday cookout, so of course there's cake. We'll go running every day next week to make up for it." He tugged Abe out of the bed and smacked his ass as he walked past. "No clothes either. I'm still pretending it's my birthday, too."

⁓

"You never take your eyes off him."

Dom turned from where he was grilling burgers, and his belly flip-flopped when he realized who'd spoken. Shane. Abe's son had been on a few hectic cases the last month, so they'd only been able to meet for lunch once since the insane shootout with James in the warehouse and even then, others had been around. Shane had watched him quietly, so obviously perplexed by Dom's relationship with his father.

After a month with the man, Dom knew even more that this was a forever thing. So Shane was just going to have to get used to him.

Coworkers and friends filled his backyard, where he'd strung lights in the trees that would come on soon with the approaching darkness. He stood on his deck, and though he was in charge of the meat portion of the meal, yeah, he'd been mostly watching Abe laughing with his boss. Abe wore those loose, sexy, and faded jeans Dom loved with a brown Henley that made his eyes look like warm coffee. Rowe made an explosion gesture with his hands and Abe threw his head back, his laughter deep and throaty.

So. Fucking. Sexy.

"Dom."

Embarrassed, he tore his gaze off his man and turned it back to the son. "Sorry."

"Actually, don't be. I'm...happy to see how you are with him. I'll confess, I came here worried. My mother did a real number on him, and he didn't date anyone again. I thought he never would. Then when he does, it's well, surprising."

"So you're thinking what? That I'm some kind of midlife crisis?"

Shane shrugged. "I was. A little." He glanced at his father, then focused brown eyes so like Abe's back on him. "But I was mostly wondering what you were after."

"After? Like his money?"

Shane looked around at the acre property and two-story house. "That's obviously not it. Looks like you do okay."

"Yeah, Ward is good to his employees." He moved a few of the burgers to the top grate and shut the lid. "Shane, I plan to ask your dad to move in here with me. I have room for a nice-sized workshop and he wouldn't have to worry about neighbors. It makes sense."

Shane smirked. "You're moving him here because you want him here."

"Of course I do." He watched Shane's face with his next words. "I'm in love with your father. Deeply, completely, and madly in love."

"I know." Shane nodded. "I can tell. Like I said, you never take your eyes off him. You look at him the way I look at Quinn—like you're wondering what the hell you ever did to land someone so wonderful." He didn't even have to look around to find his own boyfriend, his eyes zeroing in like he knew exactly where he was at all times. Quinn and several Ward employees and a few other people were sitting at the tables Dom had put under the trees. Tiki torches surrounded the yard, doing their best to drive away the mosquitos and failing. Citronella candles in buckets centered on each table were hopefully picking up the slack.

The air smelled of hamburgers, beer, and the honeysuckle growing wild across one side of his property.

Dom had strung lights in the trees and one table held a covered cake he hadn't let Abe see. Grinning at the thought of Abe's reaction to that, he flipped a couple of burgers.

Shane's attention came back to him. "Thank you for throwing him a birthday party. I'd planned to take him on that trip to the cabin last month, but he had better things to do."

"He sure did." Dom winked, then looked for Abe when laughter broke out once again. All his coworkers who were off for the night had come. Royce, Garrett, and Seth. Royce's boyfriend, Marc, sat chatting with Noah Keegan. Dom had managed to find the numbers of most of Abe's friends, too. A woman who worked at Krohn Conservatory and a few of his neighbors had come. Even the elderly lady who lived across from Abe sat next to Quinn, talking up a storm about how to kill rabid zombies in some video game.

Chuckling, Dom searched out Abe again and this time, the man was staring back at him. Their eyes locked and that swell of warmth in his chest happened again—the one that told him he'd found everything he'd always wanted in this man.

"He loves you too," Shane said. "I've never seen him this happy."

"The plan is to keep him smiling like that for the rest of his life."

"Good plan."

"I'm known for my good plans."

This time, real amusement laced Shane's laughter. "Yeah, that's not what I understand. In fact, I heard this story about a job Royce was on and some high-powered laxative…"

The heat in his cheeks suddenly had nothing to do with the grill. "Quinn is a dead man."

Snorting, Shane bent to grab a couple of beers from the cooler. He handed one to Dom. "So, about that cake."

"You peeked?"

"You already said Quinn is a dead man."

Dom shook his head, then took a swig of his beer. "He and I are gonna have a long talk."

Shane's good-natured laughter warmed his heart, but it was time for some payback.

"You know," Dom said as he scooped all of the burgers onto a plate and set it on the table next to the grill. "If I take this relationship with your father where I really want it to go, you're going to have to start calling me Daddy."

The horror on Shane's face was worth everything.

"What are you telling my son to put that look on his face?" Abe asked as he walked up behind Dom. He wrapped his arms around him and plopped his chin on Dom's shoulder.

Shane glared at him, but humor twinkled in his eyes. "He was telling me about your cake. Come on, Dad. Let's go look at it."

"Oh, good. I've been dying to see this." He tugged Dom along with him, and everyone gathered around the table as Dom grinned and lifted the cover.

Abe took one look at the cake and threw his head back, laughing.

It was a perfect cartoon replica of Dom with a purely wicked sex grin and his jeans around his ankles. A bunch of obviously picked wild flowers was held out in his hand—strategically over his crotch.

Abe's laughter choked to a stop, and he wiped his eyes as he grinned at Dom. "I should have known my *ecdysiast* would find some way to get naked at this party."

"Yeah," Dom answered. "But I only strip for you now."

FREE SHORT STORY

Don't miss out on the free short story for the Ward Security Series, JACKSON!

Wade Addams has built a new life he loves. It's far removed from the one he led as a kid under his brother's evil thumb. Forced to jack cars, he ended up in juvie. Now, ten years later, he works as a server at Rialto where he feels like part of the family.

His brother's release from prison threatens to destroy it all.

Fewer trips and time to date made Jackson Kent leave the high profile security firm he worked for in L.A. and accept the primo job offer from Ward Security. He's heard great things about the Cincinnati firm. But he never expected to meet someone like Wade his first day on the job.

Sparks fly as these two work together to keep Wade safe and send his brother back to prison where he belongs!

To download the story, go to drakeandelliott.com and click on Free Short Story in the menu bar.

CHECK OUT UNBREAKABLE BONDS

Don't miss the series that gave birth to Ward Security!

Catch up with all the action in the Unbreakable Bonds series. Now available:

Shiver
Shatter
Torch
Devour
Blaze

And the special short story collections:

Unbreakable Stories: Lucas
Unbreakable Stories: Snow
Unbreakable Stories: Rowe
Unbreakable Stories: Ian

ABOUT THE AUTHOR

Jocelynn Drake is the author of the New York Times bestselling Dark Days series and the Asylum Tales. When she's not working on a new novel or arguing with her characters, she can be found shouting at the TV while playing video games, lost in the warm embrace of a good book, or just concocting ways to torment her fellow D&D gamers. (She's an evil DM.) Jocelynn loves Bruce Wayne, Ezio Auditore, travel, tattoos, explosions, fast cars, and Anthony Bourdain. For more information about Jocelynn's world, check out www.Jocelynn-Drake.com.

Rinda Elliott is an author who loves unusual stories and credits growing up in a family of curious life-lovers who moved all over the country. Books and movies full of fantasy, science fiction, and romance kept them amused, especially in some of the stranger places. For years, she tried to separate her darker side with her humorous and romantic one. She published short fiction, but things really started happening when she gave in and mixed it up. When not lost in fiction, she loves making wine, collecting music, gaming, and spending time with her husband and two children.

She is the author of the Beri O'Dell urban fantasy series, the YA Sister of Fate Trilogy, and the paranormal romance Brothers Bernaux Trilogy. She also writes erotic fiction as Dani Worth. She can be found at www.RindaElliott.com.

Jocelynn and Rinda can be found at: www.DrakeandElliott.com.

Made in the USA
San Bernardino, CA
23 April 2019